# Feather Touch

# Feather Touch

## RAMON DHARMA RAJAN

PARTRIDGE
A Penguin Random House Company

**To order additional copies of this book, contact**
Partridge India
000 800 10062 62
orders.india@partridgepublishing.com

www.partridgepublishing.com/india

*With lots of Love forever and ever*
*To My Teachers*
*And Family*

# Acknowledgement

I see dreams crystallise before my very eyes! As I write these words, I am at the final stage of publishing my first novel. I have just faced the first big defeat of my life in the form of a failure in CA Final Exam, and just as in every story, the failure is followed by my greatest dream being realised. Here I am, with the completed manuscript and submission form, my first novel is just an email away. God is great!

My dearest Amma! Thanks a lot for telling me, "Never stop writing! No matter what you become in life, do not stop writing. It is a gift you have received and you owe it to the world." And thanks a million for not telling me, "Finish your CA first, get a job, get settled and then think about writing." Thanks for not pushing me into that nasty rat race that engulfs the youth in this country. You have inspired me to think freely, and that is just what I have done.

Dad! You have given me the most valuable thing I cherish in life. Freedom! I am not worried about a house to live in, I am not worried about food to eat or clothes to wear. You have given me complete freedom to run after my dreams and make it big. Today if I spread my wings, it is all for you, dad. Thanks for protecting me, thanks for taking care of me and thanks for loving me. And most importantly, when the uncle next door told me, "Look at that girl, she is your age only she has made an All India Rank", you told him, "At your age Rajeev Gandhi was Prime Minister!" Dad's like you can make the world a much better place.

My sweet sister – I always believe that I am person full of love. But your love for me always throws me away! My first admirer, fighter and the first person to read the novel.

In this story I have included a passage where the child recollects all his teachers. I would like to say that when I first wrote that, I had mentioned the names of my own teachers, all of them, from LKG to 12th standard. The love and support they have all given me knows no boundary and even now I know that they continue to love me. Every success of mine will be first given to my teachers at school and then to those who taught me for CA.

Suri & Co., the firm where I did my articleship holds a very special place in my heart. It is during this phase of my life that I evolved as a writer and grew mature enough to write a novel.

The only three persons whose names I will be mentioning in my acknowledgement. Rangarajan Uncle - for your guidance and mentoring, I owe you a career of writing. Akhil Nasar – Thanks a million for weaving magic on the cover design. The thoughts that you put in is nothing short of Genius.

And Mr. Damodar Narayanan! When I asked you compose a tune for this book, even I had no idea what I was talking about. It was an experiment - just a random thought. But you put your heart into that thought and created a miracle. Damoo Anna, let me tell you that if this book sells, it will be only because of your wizardry.

The biggest inspiration to this story perhaps comes from a habit which stuck with me since the age of 17 and played a huge part in moulding my thought process, up to the extent of putting the very first seeds of this novel in my brain – the habit of reading a newspaper. Full of gratitude to "The Hindu" for throwing ideas at me!

I am not a charismatic person and have countable number of friends. But the few that I have, literally form a part of my body. Two of them who deserve special mention are my heart and lungs. My lungs, whose word I take as law, and quite true to the metaphor, he supplies a lot of oxygen to my brain. And my heart, well, my life will end the minute it stops beating.

Last but not least - Thank you Partridge India for making my dream come true. My fingers tremble as I type these last words. So I guess this is it – My dream has come true!

# *Gift to the Reader*

To further enhance the experience of the reading, my cousin and I have prepared a surprise for you! So, before you start to read this book, go to <u>www.feathertouchrdr.com</u> and listen to:-

*Book* I - *Touch of the soul*

*Book* II - *Touch of the Paradise*

*Book* III - *Touch of the Feather*

These tunes are meant to augment the feel of the story so it is recommended that you listen to it as you are reading.

So... Enjoy!

*It Starts...*

Let me tell you a story...

# Feather Touch

    It took me quite a while to decide where to begin and how to begin. To follow chronology was out of the question as this story does not begin in the beginning. Much before I earned the rights to narrate I had decided that honesty would be my thumb rule and for that to happen, I will have to tell this story from my real beginning. My first day at office, my first assignment, my first trip to Earth and Kanha's birth – that is where I should start!

    Ahh... I see you were taken aback, just as I expected, at my reference to 'my first trip to Earth'. So, in the very second paragraph of my story, I am breaking my rule of an honest narration to warn you of what you are up against. In order to understand the story you will have to know who the narrator is, what his job is and why the story is being said. I am still half-hearted about it and feel that you would have enjoyed better had the story began from where I had wanted it to. But then again, I guess a little quality can be sacrificed for better comprehension. Moreover, the story has not yet begun, this is just the prologue; as a matter of fact, a pre-prologue. Here goes...

My name is Dev and I am a conscience. I was born 500 years back and completed my first life in human form forty years back, that is, I died forty years back, or in other words, my afterlife began forty years back. Still confused? Alright, I guess I have to back even further.

This is the scheme of things. Every being is brought into the universe as a soul and initially placed in a unicellular species. After that, the soul goes through twenty five reincarnations, (it was around fifty or hundred reincarnations a few centuries back, but then so much biodiversity was destroyed and the number was finally reduced to twenty five), until the soul is born as human. After the human life, begins afterlife, that is, if you were a good boy. Bad boys are reincarnated again and again in their human form until they learn; and really bad boys are sent back to the unicellular form (and the *baddest* of them will be damned to hell, but that is a myth – one of the many myths you will encounter during the course of my narration). After you successfully complete your human life, the afterlife begins. Here you have to choose a profession and serve the universe. For how long? That again is another myth, one of the myths that might prove true towards the end of the story. You will just have to wait and see. Oh! I didn't say what the myth was! They say that if you do a really good job in serving the universe, you will be blessed in heaven and… And that's it (some of the myths are taboo. Unspeakable)

I chose to serve the universe as a conscience. My job is to guide humans in their life, make sure that she remains a good girl, takes the right decisions, enjoys her life and goes to her grave 'happily ever after'. There is more to being a conscience than that, but when I started my job, this is all I knew, and it would only be right to reveal so much to you for the moment.

So, finally you know who the narrator is. Now, the story can begin... I mean, the prologue can begin.

I said good-bye to my human body as it disintegrated in its burning pyre. A really emotional scene it was, bidding farewell to the body that hosted you for over 70 years, probably the longest I lived in any life. It was a beautiful life. A happy life! A life that shaped the person I would be in afterlife, a life that truly moulded my character. I took a last look at my lifeless face and floated away with my angel of death.

My sorrow was replaced by excitement rather quickly. Life as I knew it was over – no more bodies, no more physics, I had finally entered another dimension that humans would never comprehend. I would learn of another world, the magnitude of which exponentially surpassed that of the universe humans knew of. I would finally be able to understand the scheme of nature, the reason for existence, the purpose of life and find all the answers that Buddha searched for under a tree. I had seen afterlife a number of times before (you had to check in every time you were reincarnated), but this time I was going there to stay.

I closely observed myself and my fellow angel and thought – looks like an interesting job, I have always loved travelling through the clouds into the other world; maybe I can consider this as an alternative if I get bored with being a conscience. "Such a wasteful job, sir". Oops... I forgot that souls communicate with their minds. Unlike humans, souls can't think silently. Yeah, you were wrong if you thought that a soul is some kind of superhuman with special powers who can fly around, across dimensions and read minds. Souls are handicapped in comparison to the magnificent forms of Earthly lives. "Not just that it is boring", my angel of death responded to my thought, "but there is so little scope for progress and learning. I have been doing this job for the past 100 years and only now am I allowed to cater to human deaths. And when I thought there was finally something interesting at work, I discovered that human deaths are more miserable. So much nostalgia and crap to deal with! Endless work, you have to be on the move all the time, in and out, so little time for learning. That is supposed to be the best part of afterlife, the opportunity to learn, to uncover the magnificent secrets that run the universe. What kind of learning can you have when all you do is convince people that they are dead and they have another life now? Really tired of this routine nonsense!" I wanted to disagree but no thought would go unheard, so I kept mum. Pessimism always makes me puke.

I entered the clouds and walked into what looked like a virtual room. Everything was blue and white, including me. And the colours (blue and white) mixed with each other, flowing into one another with no clear demarcation. There were no distinct shapes. All souls looked like humans but they were not solid. Many of them looked like mermaids, with a tail instead of legs, genies to be exact. Some of them adorned the looks of their favourite animals or birds – there were cats, peacocks, tigers, lions, eagles and so many others in the room.

The angel guided me through the process which resembled immigration proceedings at an airport.

"All of us are here after an earthly life so everything resembles the planet and its culture. And to be honest, the way things are run at Earth is pretty impressive. Besides all the violence and corruption, that is". The negative attitude made me itch again.

"So, what is it you want to do?" my angel asked me on behalf of one of the officers.

"Conscience", I answered. I was still not aware of the verb form of the word.

"Consciencing", my angel informed me and continued dealing with the officer. Although everything resembled Earth, the formalities didn't take much time. Apparently nothing had to be keyed into a system. "Cloud Computing" was being used extensively, as in, the cloud through which I entered collected all the data that was needed and processed it as required. There were no queues at the office and hence, everything was completed swiftly.

"You may enter that portal", the officer, who looked old with a white beard that clung from his chin, probably still in love with his good 'old' days, pointed to a tiny cubicle that looked like an escalator. "Take care and enjoy", the angel told me and I entered the cubicle. Before I could turn around, the door had closed and re-opened, revealing another office which looked so much busier and chaotic than the office I had just been in. I stepped out of the cubicle / escalator thing and saw a huge arch in front of me that read, "Conscience department".

"Now I understand the purpose of retired life", I thought to myself. "You don't have much of a holiday or a breathing space after death", the idea of getting started with my job minutes after I died struck an odd chord.

Straight ahead, sitting behind an over-crowded table, surrounded by a mob of busy souls, sat the man whom I recognized as the manager. You see, I don't have to ask anyone, "Hey, who is the manager? Can I meet the manger?" I can read minds and find out what to do. The free flow of information fascinated me.

I approached the manager who greeted me with a laugh, which he seemed to use often instead of a smile. He was a lean fellow with a small face of indistinguishable features. He gestured me "There", and I sat "There". For four years.

Four excruciatingly painful years! The purpose of retirement, breathing space bloody blundaleomite! For four tragic years I was made to sit idle on that spot! And over there I realized, an understanding that was probably a result of my over-assertive optimism, that the best way to make a man (even a soul for that matter) work with every last drop of his energy – is to make him sit idle for a period of time that will seem like "FOREVER" to him.

But I believe that I was not stupid to be optimistic. And I strongly believe that those four years of afterlife that I spent like a scarecrow; that period of time is the reason, the root cause, that I am telling you this story. "Dev", my manager called to me four years later and the vigour, with which I completed that task, continues to astonish the living day-lights out of me.

"Dev!" I remember my manager calling me in a hurried voice.

Ahh... finally, the story is about to begin. I am SO, SO Excited! Alright Dev, compose yourself. Let us get finished with the prologue now. Yeah, so my manager called for me and I was at his side in a flash. "Sir! Yes Sir!" No, I didn't say that, but that is how I picturised myself in my head.

"A baby is born. New assignment, you must go now!"

"Sir!What!?" Over the past four years I had very closely observed my colleagues at work and came to understand that the work of a conscience – Consciencing, was a demanding job that required a lot of learning and preparation. Years would go into the homework before a conscience was allotted to a person. The past, her previous incarnations, had to be thoroughly studied, the work of any previous conscience who had guided her earlier had to be looked into. 'Now' was a word, totally out of context. But before I could protest, the manager grabbed me by my hand and defenestrated me. I always manage to look at the bright side of things and I promise, the only bright side of him throwing me out of the window like that was that it gave me an opportunity to use the word "Defenestrate."

And THAT, is the end of my prologue! But you don't stop. Go ahead – Read and Enjoy!

*Book* I

# Chapter 1

# Childhood

The cries of a baby greeted my landing on Earth. I watched the doctor hand a baby boy to its mother - who looked at him with a look that no poet can describe.

Sometimes children, including myself in human life, are embarrassed by the way their mothers look at them and I have often wondered about the mystery behind that look – the way a mother looks at her child. At that moment I realized, the bliss she feels when she holds her baby for the first time, the expression gets stuck in her face and reproduces itself when the child appears - even much after the child has grown a moustache.

"Hush baby… Don't cry", Archana asked her screaming son, a strange request as I could so clearly see how much she enjoyed the noise of the boy. I looked in amazement at the mother-son duo, who was shortly joined by the father – Hari.

"Kanha", he named his son.

"Kanha's Conscience", I named myself.

The couple crooned the baby; Archana asked him not to cry and Hari began plotting his future. *"Mera Beta Engineer Banega"*, no, nobody said that, but the plans that Hari bore in his mind reminded me of that dialogue. And maybe Kanha read his mind too – his cries got louder. "Don't cry baby", Kanha's parents insisted. "Listen to your parents Kanha", I added. "Stop!" a voice echoed from above in a tone that reminded me of Shakthimaan.

"Don't advice the child yet. Just wait and observe for now. You will get further instructions tonight. Don't speak to the child till then, it could be dangerous." I recognized my manager's voice and followed his instructions. Silently, I watched the happy family.

"So, how did you like your first day at work", my manager asked me that night. For a moment I wanted to complain about having to sit idle all day and not do anything productive, but the sights I had seen during the day were overwhelming. Parents playing with the baby, singing songs and telling stories; the baby responding with surprising interest considering the literary abilities he would have developed in one day – the sights were magical. Archana lay on her husband's chest with the baby in her arms; Hari held both of them protectively; few words were passed but the trio communicated extensively. The happiness that blanketed them was almost physical – I could feel it - radiant and soothing.

"It is a special sight, I know. Must have reminded you of your own daughter." It did. "But when you observe things from this particular point of view, must have looked so much more exciting." It was indeed.

"Let's get to work then shall we?" My manager explained to me one by one what I was supposed to do. And with utmost sincerity I did it. The task at hand was to guide Kanha through his childhood, covering the various facets of that period of a person's life, starting from...

## **Kanha's Body**

"The first thing you have to do is understand his body. And ensure that everything is normal!" My manager instructed me and informed that I have an entire library for human anatomy at my disposal. "Use it well." I entered Kanha's body the very next day itself and observed it at work. I started from his mouth where food entered in the form of his mother's milk and through the oesophagus reached the stomach where a series of chemical reactions broke down milk into its constituents namely carbohydrates, proteins, fats, glucose and another bunch of vitamins and minerals. I cross checked the process with my library, a kind of in-built Wikipedia, and ensured that the chemical reactions were being done correctly. "I will get empty soon. Arrange a refill." Kanha's stomach said to the neurons which carried the message to the brain and Kanha started crying. That freaked me out. "This is something new!" I said to myself and moved on; a "just imagine it didn't happen" look on my face.

Food was taken next to the small intestine where a bunch of blood vessels sucked the nutrients and the remnants moved on to the large intestine where another filtering process happened and some amount of water was sucked up. The remaining waste was transferred to the excretory system and thrown out of the baby's body through its anus and penis.

"You have pissed again?" Archana laughed at her son. "You can exercise a little more retrain you know", the penis asked the bladder. "We are still working on it. Not as easy as it looks", the bladder responded. "This is AMAZING!" I exclaimed.

"The organs! They talk?" I asked my manager before I continued my body tour.

"Every cell does! That is why I sent you in. You are supposed to ensure that all of them do their work properly and cause no trouble. At this stage of Kanha's life, this is more important. And make sure that all of them, the cells are in good spirits, or it will affect the baby's health. Be very careful and please make sure that you report to me any sort of tension between the cells or even the organs for that matter." He hurried off.

"So I can talk to them?" He didn't respond. So I decided to experiment it. "How is work?" I asked the penis. "Ohh, not bad. A little busy actually. Could you ask the bladder to hold it a little longer?" It responded.

From then on, every day I toured the body, little by little learning the way it worked, and every day I understood that the process was mystifying. But only after Kanha joined school and I met the conscience of other students did I understand the real seriousness of things I was dealing with.

Each human body was a nation. The way it functioned was identical, with each cell representing a citizen. All the citizens worked together for the growth of the nation, and the nation in-turn ensured that its citizens lead a happy life, pulling them out of impoverishment and depravity. That was the system. Any gap in the arrangement would lead to a handicap, something I witnessed among his classmates. There were students who were stunted, obese, anaemic, asthmatic, dyslexic, and so many others. Reasons of handicap were many.

Sometimes it was due to lack in some necessary nutrient. Sometimes it was due to an unhealthy habit. Consumption of junk food often led to fat accumulation which made it difficult for blood vessels to work. Such difficulty would not be appreciated by the heart who would have to put an extra effort. A situation like that would lead to a tension between the cardio-vascular system and the digestive system and the body would have to suffer. Such ego clashes are usually resolved by the brain, but sometimes the brain itself will be involved in a conflict with the rest of the body. Or sometimes the brain is simply not competent to handle such conflict, as is mostly the case with small children who require constant attention of parents. If left unnoticed, these conflicts result in an imbalance in the functioning of the body and end up with the child's and his parents' suffering.

*It is rather quite difficult to watch school children play football, because school football is most often played in a form that resembles American football – 20 players wrestling for the ball, except that in school they wrestled with their leg and ended up kicking each other while the ball silently moves on with life. Things change if and only if there is one of those players in the team who has the prospects to become a national player. As Kanha stood at the fringes of the school playground during his break, he saw one of those players create a miracle.*

*Just before the stampede of twenty nearly trampled the ball, the tall star who was ogled at by pretty girls standing behind Kanha (in the most subtle manner; and by subtle I mean to say that not the greatest intelligence service in the world would be able to produce evidence of their eyes turning to look at the boy. But the fact that their eyes did turn and their hearts were full of that sight alone is something this conscience can vouch for). The fair, thin, tall boy with a bright face that gleamed with sweat, wearing a lose shirt struggled to catch up with him as he raced the wind, that flew behind him in the most charismatic style, directed the ball away from the mob and towards the opposite goal. And while the girls almost fainted at the look of focus and determination in his eyes (which was genuine... What is not genuine is the fact that he carries the same look even outside the field. I call it "attitude, aka, one of the thousand ways to make girls look at you"), 5 year old Kanha admired the way the 12th grader moved across the length of the green field.*

*Just outside the grassy football ground which opened up to a road that lead to the school on one side and was surrounded by brilliant trees on the other tree, Kanha sat under a banyan tree, his eyes taking in the sight with awe. The muscles in his limbs tingled as he saw the tall footballer swiftly sprint from one point to another at one time and then go one a streak from one corner to the other almost as if the wind carried him. "Let's do that!" His legs cried.*

*"The others will think you are mad if they see you running like that simply", the brain chided.*

*"No matter. It must be so nice! Just kicking the ground away and leaping forward. Like a stag in the grassland. So majestic, so temping!" And so spoke thousands of cells in his legs. The tissues resonated*

the voice with much stress that was then forwarded to the muscles and then passed on to the brain through a neuron. The brain received this message along with the testimony of the eyes that were mesmerised by the sight and the approval of the nose which loved the fresh air and the skin which hoped for wind to blow against it and cool itself. The brain however had its reservations with respect to the worries that his classmates might make fun of him and the energy constraint in his body. And neither was the brain too confident about strength its muscular system had in it. However, subdued by the overwhelming internal pressure, the democratic brain succumbed to the demands of its citizens and decided to have a jog.

One leap forward and then another, "Oh man! I want to run like that boy! I want to kick the ball around and have everyone else eat dust. I want to fly like him", various cells echoed in his body, overwhelmed with themselves as young Kanha bounced forward.

*Crash* As the star footballer trebled through the defence of his opponents, a frustrated player stretched his leg forward, tripping the boy and ending his deadly spree with a violent fall on the ground with his back hitting the grass in a "thud"!

The bones in Kanha's body flinched. "Hey, wait! This is too dangerous. Painful!"

The boy struggled to get up. He slowly raised his hand and displayed a bloodied arm and torn skin. "No! This is not worth the risk!"

"Hey, it won't hurt that bad?" the muscles tried to console.

"We can't sacrifice Kanha's health just for one organ. It is wiser to stay put. Let's go and study!"

*Kanha, walked towards the tree where he had kept his bag, pulled out a book and started studying.*

Each child's body functioned differently. Some bodies had capitalistic attitude, where the organs would perform efficiently for the body even if the cells were not content. Such children would excel in class but their conscience testify that their parents weren't always in good health. Sometimes the cells would be adamant and the organ would have to give in to its demand. Such situations resulted in conflicts, but with the help of an active brain and under the guidance of an experienced conscience, things would be sorted out and everything will be happily ever after.

Such revelations by fellow conscience often tense me up and I go on another round of inspection to make sure that everything was alright. And thankfully, so far there have been no flaws in Kanha's system. All through childhood he was healthy and his citizens never complained. As a matter of fact, they were always content. And except for the first week, his bladder could hold out for a really long time and even the cells on night duty worked hard. However, this is just about his childhood. What happened after that? You will read about it soon. But before that there is so much more to Kanha's childhood, his parents, his school, teachers, friends, studies, exams, his dearest Radha and most important of all – his obsession with obedience.

## **Obsession**

I like to believe that it is not my fault, but simply can't get the thought out of my head. My manager says that any advice given to a baby is likely to have an amplified effect – my very first advice, "Listen to your parents", for instance. Just as I said that to him, Kanha stopped crying, and since then he has been a very obedient child, something his parents can be proud of and something that has reduced my workload by tons. As a toddler Kanha caused no trouble, went about to no mischief and was truly a model child for the neighbourhood, a fact that Archana and Hari couldn't praise enough. Even if it meant that everything they said was taken literally and he would remain so unless he was told to do something else.

Now this adherence with obedience made him different from other children who explored anything and everything, venturing into a realm of curiosity at every opportunity they could grab. This was a small issue that worried me, but things got out of control when obedience evolved into obsession and as he grew up, the brain re-tuned an re-wired itself making Kanha obey several contrasting commands issued by his parents in an optimal manner. Now a mother, or any adult doesn't exactly issue commands, I know, but Kanha never understood the difference and he listened to them with military discipline.

On one hand they asked him to be careful in the play ground and on the other they would say that daily exercise is very important for growth. His teachers advised that games are the best form of exercise, and at his playground it would be evident that it is not exactly possible to play a game and be very safe at the same time. In such situations the brain worked like a computer on the basis of a set of in-built rules, protocol and hierarchy. Parents always came first and his mother had precedence over his father, and parents over his teachers. And if his mother happened to say something contradictory, he would follow FIFO basis and her first command had precedence.

Thus, Kanha grew up to be a really studious child who showed absolutely no interest in sports or games.

Sometimes the obsession would back-fire with un-savoury results; like the one time the family went to a temple and had to wait at a long queue. The only one instance throughout his childhood (that is, from birth to class X) that I saw him lose his temper.

*Kanha's obsession reached a fever top and he disobeyed his parents. He simply couldn't understand the purpose of standing queue in between sweaty shirtless men to see a statue in which he had little faith, instead of preparing for exams where he was instructed (or commanded, as he saw it), by so many to get first rank. He saw the wait as a blasphemous time kill and the cells in his body were patriotic citizens in their reaction. "We don't want anything that harms our nation", his body echoed and rose with protest. His leg muscles went weak, the stomach went empty and the bladder refused to hold it any longer.*

*"Dad, I can't stand it any longer!" Kanha complained desperately. But his father would pay no heed. "You are a big boy Kanha. Just wait a little longer", "Don't behave like this Kanha. This is a very holy place, you should be respectful", his parents responded. "This place isn't holy! It is a waste of time, money and energy! A toilet is more important at the moment", Kanha had*

*just turned thirteen then and the advent of teenage brought in a rebel with it. Until… SLAP!*

*No, it wasn't so loud, Hari wouldn't slap his precious son at a temple, in front of so many people. But his hand did fall on Kanha's cheeks and it burned him. Things almost went out of control when I rushed to the scene.*

*In a dash I went around his body and talked to all the organs, assuring them that rebellion was not in Kanha's best interest. After convincing his bladder to hold in longer and giving strength to his legs I advised Kanha about the significance of his wait. I whispered to him about the importance of being patient and calm in such situations. I pumped his spirit with optimism and told him to have faith in his parents and the fact that if they believed the temple visit was good for him, they might be right. "When have they ever done something that could hurt you. Trust your parents as you always do." I advised. And he listened to half of it, barely convinced.*

*"You know this temple has a lot of historic importance", I played my trump card and that found its mark! Kanha looked around at the sculptures and the paintings on the walls with curiosity and interest. "Nerds are rather easy to trick!" I told myself and reclined.*

Little did I know that the stint of rebellion I had seen was just the beginning of a hostile turn his obsession would take.

## Parents

Hari, Kanha's father, was fair, tall man who worked as the accounts manager at a software company in

Thiruvananthapuram and Archana was a housewife. The family lived in an apartment at Vazhuthacaud which was bought an year before Kanha was born. Kanha's maternal grandparents lived in Ambalapuzha, a lush green town situated in mid-Kerala and the paternal counterparts lived in Kottayam city, in spite of repeated invites by Hari asking them to live with the family.

Yes, Hari asked his parents to live with them, he was a gentleman. A man with principles, a man who could easily become a role model for his son – no smoking, no drinking; an educated fellow who lived a simple and dignified life. He was 6 feet tall, with an almost cubical face and a receding hairline that had just started greying when Kanha was born. And he wanted Kanha to be exactly like him, a wish that came true except, and much to his happiness, the looks.

Besides the cubical face, Kanha resembled his mother Archana, who had a really small face and pretty features. In sharp contrast to her husband she was lean and just above 5 feet tall, with thick hair that also covered her forehead. She most often wore a sari, even at home, and had an eternally youthful look.

And unlike Hari, she had no schemes or plans for her son. Just a simple wish – he should always be happy. And safe (mothers think of nothing else)! The father however had several plans; he wanted Kanha to be very well educated and lead a scholarly life. Kanha must uphold the dignity of the family in terms of knowledge and honour. "Be a role model for everyone", Hari would tell his son from time to time and Kanha took these words of wisdom as strict commands and made no mistake in abiding them.

So much that Kanha's childhood dreams were filled with the image of Mr. Perfect! If obedience was his obsession, obeying that one instruction by his father was his greatest ambition and deepest passion – two strong words for a 5 year old. But that was the truth. He dreamt of being a perfect man who would be loved and admired by all.

An admirable trait for a young boy, but ambition must always be handled with maturity, and Kanha was way too young for that. As he grew older, high school to be precise, he became fanatic about his ambition; his desire to be the "Mr. Perfect" clouded every other thought in his brain.

It was a happy family that earned the envy of every other house in the apartment building. They played caroms every night, shared stories with each other, boasted of success and achievements – father at work and son at school. But as I said earlier, high-school took a nasty turn, one that I tried to avoid, with little success. The daily game of caroms stopped, and Kanha's presence outside his study room decreased. His parents attributed this to the pressure of Board exams and didn't complain, but the problem was a serious one. One they should have complained about.

## <u>School</u>

Kanha's early school days were a golden age for him. Success and admiration blanketed him. Teachers loved him. "Learn something from Kanha", was a regular phrase in classroom. Every competition (except sports), featured Kanha's name on top of the winner's chart.

Kanha too loved his school and to this day, if somebody asked him to speak about his success in life, this paragraph would not fail to be a part of his speech.

"Any success I achieved in life can firstly be attributed to the fact that I know to read and write, and for that I will be forever indebted to Mrs. Devika Nair, the wonderful woman who taught me the English and Hind Alphabets in Kindergarten. School was a blissful experience and childhood is filled with fascinating memories, thanks a lot to Rakhi teacher and Anuja Das teacher, my class teachers in first standard. A wonderful teacher, who continued to guide me as a teacher and a family friend much after I finished class two, Suhana Teacher. I still remember being taught the planetary movements by Praseethi Shyam teacher in class three and the admirable accent of my then English teacher, Reshma Maam. And my favourite of them all would be Nasreen Maam who taught me mathematics in class four, whose constant appreciation for me took my confidence to new levels. Hindi teacher Mehra Maam's encouragement, social studies teacher Sohail sir's love and affection and fifth standard class teacher Neethu Gupta Maam's strictness, though sweet words did slip out are still fresh in my memory.

"Sixth standard class teacher Tarun Kumar sir, whose favourite student was me, Saroj sir, who abhorred the administrative policies of George Bush, Wahid Sir who taught me social studies, or I might even say made me hope to become an archeologist one day, Deepthi Singh Maam, whose knowledge of History and Geography kept me spell bound, Maths teacher Thomas sir who always kept his classroom in good spirits and so many more are a constant source of inspiration for me. The most beautiful Divya Maam makes me nostalgic about class 7. Malayalam Teacher Sanusha Maam, I refuse to admit that she is a teacher. She is a 'Super-Teacher'. Her methods were… Perfect.

"High-school, where the pressure of board exams might choke a student, a number of amazing angels kept me afloat! Akbar sir, class nine social studies, George sir, class nine mathematics and Johnson sir for chemistry were more of friends than teachers. Priya Maam who taught me biology, didn't just teach me about the human body but also appraised my character with remarkable accuracy. Kevin sir, who would give me a tight hug, like no other friend of mine would. Aswathy Maam, who tutored me in English and, let's just say, turned the exam into a cake-walk. Aravindan Sir, whom I consider second to Shakuntala Devi and Sridevi Maam, whose words, 'Go and Shine. Make us proud' still fuel me. And the most Amazing Shoshamma Teacher, in whose classroom about Vaikkom Mohammed Basheer I took a resolve to write at least one novel!"

The speech goes on singing concerts of praise for his 11th and 12th standard teacher – Smitha Miss for constant support for participation of extra-curricular activities, Swathy Maam, who made accountancy his favourite subject, Bhavana Miss, who took his marks in mathematics from 59 to 95, Jayanthi Miss, whom he and his peers loved like their own classmate, Merin Thomas teacher who took 'logical application of mind' to the next level in class, Merin Jacob Miss who gave him the opportunity to write his first script and present it in class (only I know what a disaster that turned into. You will read of it soon), Shreya Miss, whose touching words in his slam book still make him emotional,

Jessina miss who worked so hard in her classes and Aruna Miss, whose guidance and support went long after school got over.

The way Kanha dealt with his school life was indeed artistic, something to learn from. And this statement comes from a conscience, who is supposed to teach humans. In the very first day itself, a combination of his obedience and discipline, and absence of fear made him stand out. He sat at his place throughout the day while 25 others of his age cried their lungs out. While peer pressure made kids do really awful things, especially during teenage, Kanha was not even aware of the things that happened in the underground of his school.

*As the sun rose, buses would start from the premises of Kanha's school and as morning star pours itself in all glory of the day, the three story building would get filled with the amazing "future of the world"*

*Inspite of hosting the most notorious species in the planet – children, the building was quite neat and tidy, and until the students began to fill the classrooms, the chairs and tables would be in order. The school was a single three storied building having around 70 classrooms besides an auditorium in the 3$^{rd}$ floor, and four laboratories and separate playgrounds for football, basketball, volley-ball and the kids' play area. The walls were decorated with charts prepared by the students themselves, showing off to the world the magnificent wonders of science, history and art, the canteen was always packed with snacks, including junk food (because even a temple has to make profits), the* *local book-store always bore the beautiful smell of new books, the staffrooms were reminiscent of the fears that students carried with them as they walked past it, the toilets were impaired beyond repair (especially the kindergarden toilet, but no complaints there) and the classrooms continue to make men and women speechless with nostalgia. The hours one spends each day for the first fourteen years of life and the memories one carries in each of those seconds, the voices that are imprinted in ears as if on stone, the blackboard that is fresh in every person's eye forever and ever, the smell of chalk-powder, the sound of chalk and duster on the board followed by that of pens or pencils on the book. Notebooks being piled up on the teacher's table at the end of the day and being returned after the bathe in red ink the next day – every molecule of air in the class had all of this to offer the five senses. All of this and much, much more!*

*The classroom could comfortably accommodate 40 students that was split into 8 benches, 4 on each side of the class. The teachers ensured that boys and girls sat next to each other as a part of the school culture and in an attempt to ensure that nobody shied away from their peers.*

*"Define Valency!" the teacher asked to the classroom which was buzzing until then. Until the teacher wrote those 7 letters on the board there was this persistent chat in the room, nobody knew who spoke, nobody knew who made the noise, and to be honest, nobody including myself heard that voice except the teacher herself. And every now and then it made her turn around and ask, "Who is talking over there?", or,*

*"If you are not interested please get out of the class!" Sometimes when the buzz was indeed audible she would say, "I have never seen such a class ever in my life!" I find it strange that in my human life, even when I attended school, the teacher said the same thing.*

*However, this teacher knew her job and hence came up with the best of tactics to silence the class. A question like that and a 'look' at 40 faces would ensure that no word was uttered until the class got over.*

*At that moment, the teacher began a game of supreme mind play that any adult in the outside world would instantaneously fail at. Only those 7th grade students would be able to bear the brunt of that mind play which the teacher would unleash upon them. A combination of a diabolic stare and the sound of the cane tapping on her palm would bring sweat on the face of any student who had the slightest doubts on their confidence. Some students took it to extremes by completely avoiding her face, but their faces couldn't hide the fear, they would be held up. Another lot wouldn't even bother to look away, but the fear would petrify them right away and they would end up staring at the teacher's face, helplessly. Then of course there would be those who knew the answer very well (just so few of them), whose faces would be brimming with confidence. They would be picked up only if the teacher was in a mood to be pleased. And then those who could fake the confidence. They would do really well in life… for a very short while.*

*Kanha happened to be in the third category, a shining face waiting to pop out the answer. And Radha happened to be in the first category, a depressed face was what she bore, but little did anyone know that it was ignorance which gave made her depressed. The teacher noticed a little dark girl in a corner of the classroom seeming completely lost. She was smaller than the others of her age, her hair was curly and looked… odd. "Radha stand up!" The teacher commanded.*

*The startled girl stood up and looked at the teacher with a timid face. "Mm", the teacher nodded towards the board where she had written the question, "define valency!" And as if she was asked to sing a song, or more like a nursery rhyme, the little girl popped into a smile and gave the answer flawlessly. The entire answer, of which not one word I understood, was spit out in 23 seconds which made the teacher drop her jaw. She didn't admit her astonishment though, obviously.*

The things that gave nightmares to most students were deftly handled by the boy. Assignments were completed well before the due date, homework was never delayed and he never forgot to take the textbook to class. And each exam was tackled in a team effort put by the mother and son. Studies were completed weeks before the exam and there would be 2-3 revisions for each subject, plus another round of preparations for lessons in which he was weak.

Yet the day of results gave him goose bumps. His hands would shiver and turn as cold as ice. Restlessness and tension would engulf him and Kanha would be seen running up and down his apartment building. No friend could comfort him, no adult could console him, the pressure would ease only when the report card was handed to him and he saw the "Full A+".

And unlike other students, Kanha's report card shows a steady graph till class ten. Every year the routine icing of hands and restlessness would happen, and every year the marks would earn the envy of neighbours. And the effort put by him increased with every passing year. Till class 10.

## **Friends**

Everyday his teachers bathed him with adulations, but Kanha did not have the charisma to gain the same from him peers. He wasn't the centre of attraction in his class and his dislike to sports did not win him any respect. But still he had friends, a bunch of boys and girls who hung out with him during break-hours and sometimes chatted after school too. And more importantly, nobody disliked Kanha. Everybody was just neutral towards him. Throughout primary school.

*"I was just wondering how this guy must be doing his business in the morning?" Rajkumar asked his friends over lunch.*

*"What business?"*

*"I meant shitting! I mean, would he still have a book in his hand. Probably a pen and a pencil over there too… working out a sum in Maths as his butt went on to do its work?" The two of them laughed at their own conversation.*

*"I seriously pity him, yaar. He does not have a life at all. Video games, cartoons, sports, none of that!" The second guy, I guess his name was Vineeth, remarked.*

*"I seriously hate that guy. So much attitude! He doesn't talk to anyone at all. Except that girl named*

*Radha! Ughh… that's another creature!" I was aghast at that remark.*

*"Hahh… Birds of a feather flock together. Radha is annoying", I have no idea why he said that – she is an angel, "but this fellow is kind of ok. I mean, he doesn't come over to irritate you."*

*"Even that girl doesn't come over or anything."*

*"Yeah, I know… but there is something about her that is… She looks so… I don't know…" Nobody knew. Some things have no reason.*

But as I said before, Kanha's obsession and ambition took a violent and hostile turn as he stepped into high school. As the teachers made it evident about the impending disaster namely Board Exams and hopes soared high regarding Kanha's performance, his body and mind became wholly engrossed with the preparations for exams. He ditched his friends. And started avoiding everyone else.

A conscience only guides the human, we can't command. Even a person like Kanha may obey only if he wants to. But the turn of events during his high school were such that I used all my force to change him. I campaigned extensively within his body and appealed to his mind, but Kanha paid no heed. He wouldn't listen to his conscience. I talked to his parents' conscience and tried convincing Hari and Archana to ask their son not to be engrossed in such an unhealthy manner. They too didn't listen. The boards took its toll on the child.

The most worrying thing about it was that some cells in his body were not pleased with his attitude. He had completely given up exercise or any physical activity for that matter and this earned him mixed reaction from within his body. While some organs supported him some of his muscles, for instance, which grew lazy and encouraged him to sit at one place for a longer time, while some of his muscles expressed their displeasure by growing restless and demanding some movement and activity. His eyes were diligently at work and supported him without complains while his digestive system was opposed to his ways and protested with their excessive and frequent demands.

However, Kanha made optimum use of his supporters, and crushed the opponents with his will power. I was confused and didn't know what to do, only hoped that things would reconcile once the exams got over.

Having said all that, Kanha's alienation from his parents, the ire he earned from his peers, the conflict that was brewing in his body, I assert that the biggest loss of all was one special person who too was ignored along with his other friends. Everything else that he did were mistakes in my point of view, but this one was a crime. Radha deserved better.

## **Radha**

*"I woke up in the morning at exactly four o' clock just as Amma told me to, brushed my teeth, had a bath, said my prayers and came down to have breakfast. Amma had prepared dosa today, with red colour chutney. The chutney was too spicy and I asked her for the while colour chutney but Amma said that I am a big girl now and that I should get used to eating all this. I did not like it that much, but ate two full dosas.*

*After that, my Appa helped me get dressed up and at exactly at 6 o' clock I was waiting outside my house for the bus. The bus was late by five minutes as usual and this irritated Appa. He is a very punctual man. But I did not complaint. Whenever I get inside the bus some of the boys and girls start teasing me saying this and that and it makes me sad. Sometimes I feel so sad that I keep praying the bus shouldn't come at all, but today I was not that scared. When I got into the bus one of the boys commented, "Hey, springy hair!" and the others laughed. I ignored them and went to sit in the second last window seat. Then on the journey was comfortable, I love the sights outside the bus.*

*"Then I reached school. There was a test in the first period which was very easy. I was pretty sure only that I wrote all the answers correctly but any case, Kanha came over to my bench to discuss the answers after the test and we confirmed that both of us had got everything correct. Then he went back to his seat. I wished he would give me company but he had some book to read, so he didn't talk to me much. I also picked up the story book I had borrowed from the library and started reading it. It was fun.*

*"Class got over and I came home. Amma gave me lunch and then I had a nap for an hour. I woke up and did my homework, there wasn't much today. After that I revised all that was taught today.*

*"Evening Appa came back on time and he played with me as soon as he came back. I was looking forward to that all day, especially because Kanha said he won't be coming to my house today and said he was busy. But he was very tired so he didn't play for very long. I also felt sorry for him and asked him to take rest.*

*At night we had idly. Amma makes the softest idlys in the world. And there was white chutney too. At night I saw a cartoon about a detective dog and his friends who fight ghosts. I am a brave girl, I am not afraid of ghosts. And then I went to sleep. Good night"*

- *10 year old Radha's diary read.*

Kanha's best friend. Bestest friends forever! Kanha never showed that he had any such emotional inclination, but Radha was very much attached to him and made it evident. True that she had few friends, as a matter of fact, no friends at all except him, but the way she kept her friendship was admirable no matter what. To all the students of their school, I would only say that they have made a huge loss by ignoring her. A girl who loves her friend with all her heart and would go through any hell to protect that love."Hey, there's something on your head?" That was the first thing Kanha ever said to her when they were in first standard.

P.E. periods were not something Kanha looked forward to, given his dislike for sports and that is when he noticed a little girl, quite small for her age and whose skin tone was a dark shade of brown, sitting outside the playground watching her friends at play. Kanha had seen her before in class and knew that she was a bright child (I refuse to believe that her brilliance in studies was the reason he decided to befriend her, but I think it is the truth), and he approached her during one such P.E. periods.

"Huh?" Radha seemed to be startled to see him. "Something on your head", Kanha repeated and brushed a little feather off her boy-cut hair. Radha did look kind of awkward in her school uniform, neatly pressed and glowing white, which in turn brought out her own darkness.

"Thanks", she smiled and continued "Aren't you playing?" And she asked that with a lot of confidence. I have to admit that she was not the prettiest girl but when she smiled, her smile had a glow in it and that was beautiful to look at. I decided that I had to talk to her conscience to ask her to smile more often.

"Oh! No, I don't like playing", apparently Kanha too was taken aback by her confidence. Probably he too was expecting a shy response.

There was an awkward silence between them for a moment. "Ask her why she isn't playing!", I told Kanha. "Why aren't you playing? Don't you like it?" Kanha listened to me.

"Umm… actually I do. But they don't let me play." Why of course, there is one outcaste in every class. So sad that such a beautiful kid was the victim in that class. "It is because I don't look so good", she added without rubbing the smile off her face.

Radha didn't grow up to be a hot chick, but her smile grew prettier every day. And every day since then she gifted Kanha with her smile. Kanha too liked her presence. And oddly enough, she always had a feather stuck to her head.

Everyday after school Kanha would rush to Radha's house which happened to be in the very next building and they would hang out, playing a game or doing their homework together. And if Kanha was not in the mood to go out, or had some extra studying to do, Radha walked over to his house. And they talked a lot. Rather mature discussion for their age I would say.

They discussed about school, about homework, shared general knowledge, solved puzzles, played caroms or chess and finally when they were out of activity, they would watch T.V. Kanha didn't like cartoons, he considered them to be a waste of time, so they watched news, which either of them understood very little of, but still watched because it gave them an adult aura. And Kanha liked telling others at school what he saw on news the previous day.

Like silly friends they had fights too, most of which were started by Kanha and ended by Radha. Very often, she would apologize for a fault that was entirely Kanha's and Kanha would forgive her after giving it a serious thought. But sometimes Kanha took it too far by not talking to her for a day or two, and when Radha would come looking for him, he would refuse to see her, or simply choose to hang out with some other kids from the building or any of his school friends. But none of these fights lasted for more than a day, as Kanha (I would say Nobody), could stay angry at Radha longer than that.

*"Kanha was very angry at me today. We had discussed the entire question paper and our answers matched but when the results came he lost half a mark because of a silly mistake. But still he was class second, and the one who got class third got only 8 marks, but he was very angry because I got full correct and became class first. For the past few days he had not come over to my house, I don't know why, but I was hoping he would come over to my house today, but that isn't likely to happen. I wish I had made that mistake too. He would still be a little angry but not like*

*this. I told him sorry but he isn't talking to me. During lunch break I went over and told him sorry again, but he walked off his seat and went to talk with some of his other friends. I went back in my seat. I felt a little sad but I know he will forget all of this tomorrow and we will be best friends again", she was smiling as she wrote that in her diary. But Kanha, didn't talk to her the next day also. Only the day after that did Radha go to his house saying she had a few doubts and asking his help. Half heartedly he said ok. At the end of the day, Kanha had forgotten everything.*

As they grew older and boy-girl relationships started becoming more than just friendships, the Kanha-Radha gossip stories were quick to release. Their names didn't help dodging the tease either. "Krishna and Radha go on flirting forever", "No wonder they never play with us. They have better things to do!" And such mockery got high on Kanha's nerves. But even then, I didn't have to interfere; Radha acted as a better conscience to Kanha than me. "Cool down Kanha, they are just saying this for fun. Ignore it", and Kanha struggled to obey her (in his hierarchy of obedience, Radha had a very low rank).

Their rivalry in exams also is a fascinating story. Kanha always came first and Radha always came second. - The End –

But like every other relationship, Kanha cut her off too. "Have to focus on studies. Have to beat the Boards", Kanha told her and didn't talk to her for two years.

"Must be best for him. I will let him be if that is what he wants", Radha told herself and withdrew the scene with grace. "No! DON'T!" I cried.

And what happened to the much talked about board exams. Kanha aced it! As expected. And thus ended Kanha's childhood. But what was not expected was what happened after his childhood. After tenth Standard.

# Chapter 2

# Invasion

Her eyes were like swans swimming in crystal clear water, as she blinked, the swan seemed to flap its wings, sending a subtle simmer in the lake. Her hair was most often tied in a ponytail that reached well below her shoulders, but occasionally a tuft would fall on her face. That was a face that turned many boys into poets. It was the face that made Kanha fall in love.

But before I get to that part of the story I must inform you of the Battle of Plassey that happened in Kanha's body and other waves of changes that hit him like a train. Kanha was a bookworm all through childhood and his body, although several parts preferred a more athletic routine, did not complain and, as a matter of fact, thoroughly supported him in his academic conquests. The fanatic approach he took in high-school, however, did not go well with his body. And when they objected, Kanha crushed them with his will power. His muscles yearned for exercise, a brisk stroll outside his apartment at least, but a firm 'No' was Kanha's response.

And Kanha did succeed in exercising control over his body, except for one aspect – puberty! A feathery hairline had appeared below his nose and marked its more dominant presence in other parts of his body too. As Kanha immersed himself in his books, his penis grew erect and his balls dropped.

Puberty, for Kanha, was more than just a biological development – it was a political invasion in Kanha's body. A gradual shift of power was happening, from the brain to the testicles, from the nervous system to his reproductive system. As the unrest enlarged in his body, the cells began to accept a new leader for themselves. Silently through hectic schedule of board exam preparations, the brain was reduced to a king who sat on his throne – and commanded nobody.

School re-opened, a new student joined school – Chandrika: The brain was officially dethroned.

Kanha could not believe what was happening to him. He couldn't resist the urge to ogle at her. The teacher would explain in class, but ears refused to carry the message, the brain refused to register anything but the voice of Chandrika. His heart treasured her words that he heard from across the classroom. Not across the classroom exactly, both of them sat in the front row, Kanha in the right edge and Chandrika in the left, making them sit close to each other. His hands trembled because of her presence.

The revolt of 1857 was going on in his head:-

"This is absolutely ridiculous! I have ambitions to chase, dreams to follow, a world to change! I can't fall in love – I don't have time for girls."

"Love is what runs the universe and falling in love is not a crime. Love will not stop you from chasing your dreams, it will only fire them up."

"I don't have the kind of time to pay attention to girls. And she isn't the type of girls who will even understand what I am up to!"

Oooo.... What is he upto now? I know that the story is in an important juncture and this is the worst time to digress, but there is a little secret that Kanha had been keeping, something of which only I knew!

"Rajaram Mohan Roy, Swami Vivekandanda, Mohandas Karamchand Gandhi, Sardar Vallabhai Patel, B.R.Ambedkar, Maulana Abdul Kalam Azad, Jawaharlal Nehru, Rabindranath Tagore – these are not just names of freedom fighters; they are heroes who changed the world. These are people an entire generation looked at with awe and generations to follow will continue to do so. Nobody can stop singing praises for them, the perfect gentlemen!'

"They had nothing else in mind besides the mission they had dedicated themselves to achieve. They saw nothing but the parrot's eye. And that vision of theirs – changed the world!" Thus went the speech given by Kanha's school principal in his fifth standard. Had I not mentioned to you earlier about how Kanha's obsession for obedience had turned into a passion to become perfect? This passion, much due to the influence of his Principal's words, went another step further into a fiery ambition. An ambition to "Change The World!"

This was one miniscule aspect of his childhood that I had missed out in my narrative, but I guess this also is a suitable time to mention it. However, coming back to the revolt of 1857:

"I have a dream, and you know how fanatically I am chasing it." Kanha refers to himself as you when such conflicts happen in his head. He continued fighting himself, "Every year I try to go the extra mile, pushing my limits to the farthest. I have come too far. Can't stop now!"

But his balls were way ahead. They had manipulated his brain to make him say this, "All these great men loved what they did. They LOVED! How can you do what they did if you don't even know what love is? How can you feel their intensity? Their fire!

"Mahakavi Ulloor S Parameswar Iyear has said, that love is the one true religion, one true science and one true God. Love is gravity. There is love in everything. And you haven't had the feel of it yet."

As these arguments began to convince Kanha, his penis too began to grow. He has previously, and he could continue to, overcome the temptations of his upcoming adult life, but the invasion in his brain and proven to be a formidable force. Thus, a coup had taken place.

"I am in love", Kanha admitted to himself, and his entire body rejoiced at the political success that had been achieved.

And the success did yield quick dividends. As love flooded his heart, textbooks were closed and the MP3 player was turned on. Songs were downloaded, the most romantic ones of the season and his ears were soothed all night. His limbs that craved athletic activity couldn't stop waltzing as Kanha drifted into a dream world. His neurons too relished their holiday in the thoughts of the angel Kanha had fallen in love with.

And his testicles celebrated their success with a wild round of masturbation.

Morning, Kanha was Raj, afternoon he was Rahul and at night he was... (I am trying to tell a family story here you know. And I am editing off that metaphor). Movies and music had drugged his brain, irrespective of language, irrespective of character, all that mattered was that mystical emotion that literally created magic. Literally!

And what did I feel about all that? I was kind of happy for him, happy that he was no longer fanatic about his... (Shhh... he doesn't like it when I mention that ambition), his studies. He smiled more often, started playing caroms with his parents again, and hung out with his neighbours. His body was in sync with his mind and both of them were happy. What else could a conscience want? A few things more.

First of all, I wanted Kanha to pay a little more attention to his studies (I never, never ever, thought I would have to say that!). A couple of months had passed since school started and his first mid-term exams were due in a week, and the boy had not yet opened his books. 15 years of training as a conscience had taught me that I had to be far-sighted and the way Kanha went forward with his studies meant a lot of trouble. There was solace in the fact that being studious was in his genes. Or as some might say, in his destiny! Kanha was a big boy and knew his responsibilities very well. I didn't feel I had to run around him with advices or ask his parents to advice him. But I was still worried.

Second of all, he continued to ignore Radha. I talked to him about this and in one of those rare occasions where he was bored, he heard his conscience. "You have to talk to Radha. She is your best friend", I told him.

"Not in the mood for it. I can't talk to Radha if all I can think about it Chandrika!" Kanha said and returned to his music.

Since class XI began, the two of them didn't see much of each other either, as Kanha had opted for commerce and Chandrika was in science. And whenever they passed each other, the way they behaved made me scream, "COMPLETE STRANGERS ARE BETTER THAN THAT!" Ignoring somebody is something. The two of them barely acknowledged the others' existence in the universe.

And Radha behaving like that too!? That gave me a serious shock. I had expected her to come running up to the flat the day exams got over. I had hoped to make Kanha take a break during his summer vacations (instead of scheming for his… unspeakable things). But Radha didn't show up and Kanha sat in his bedroom staring at the sky (which made me wonder whether he was too ambitious, or simply drugged!)

"Why is she like that?" Finally, one day I got the opportunity to ask Lakshmi – Radha's conscience.

"It is all your fault!"

"What me?" I had slipped out of the house after Kanha had fallen asleep and managed to find Lakhmi hovering above the Radha's apartment building. She too seemed to be deep in thought and worry.

"Yes, you! What kind of conscience are you, letting your person behave so brutally!" Lakshmi told me angrily.

"Hey, we have had this discussion before and I have told you the kind of person Kanha is. He is fanatic about his studies."

"During summer vacations?"

"He was always reading", that wasn't a complete lie, he did a lot of reading too. "I thought Radha would come over and help me out with things. I am afraid it might become dangerous!"

"Afraid? Might become? Things have gone out of control already with Radha over here. Oh my god! It is too bad."

"What happened?" I didn't have to ask.

"Loneliness finally got the best of her. She is depressed now. Totally!" Lakhmi explained with a tear falling on her blue cheeks. "The way her vacations got through, I couldn't bear the sights. Solitude took a cruel grip on her. Every day she expected Kanha to come knocking at the door. Or at least call her", Lakshmi burst out and continued with sobs.

"Throughout the board exams she had been waiting for a chance to get back with Kanha. She had taken a firm resolve of not interrupting him with his studies till the exams got over. But the minute after it did, she wanted to talk to him. But that day she couldn't. The day exams got over Kanha rushed out of the exam hall without a word to anybody." I remembered that day. He had ran out of the exam hall for fear that his friends might invite him to a celebration or something. Kanha had decided during his exams itself that for summer vacations he would be even more busy at "work" (I am talking about the aforementioned 'scheme', if you know what I mean).

"That made her upset and she decided to wait until Kanha called her. That night she slept hoping to get his call, he didn't call. The next morning she woke up before the sun, had a bath and was ready at the kitchen to help her mother out like every other day. However, the sound of the lightest 'TAP' made her flinch and rush towards the door. And the routine continued every day during the summer vacation. When there was no work to be done, she would sit in her room reading some book, and having imaginary discussions with Kanha about the book. 'The story was a bit dull, I agree, but the way he narrated it was simply too good!' she would say. 'Why would anyone read a book for the way it is narrated? Does the book send a message? Does it have a moral? Will it change people's minds? That is what matters!' she imagined Kanha saying.

"Similar conversations would take place as she watched the news channels on T.V. And whenever she caught a glimpse of the cartoon channels, she would mimic Kanha's expression of disgust.

"Then school re-opened, where she finally reconciled to the fact that Kanha was not going to talk to her. She grew accustomed to it. But the fact that she continued to be the outcaste in her class – that shook her violently.

"Still? I mean, with so many new students joining the school?"

"Most of her classmates are the old ones. And the new ones too are under that influence."

"Being an outcaste in primary school is understandable, but in class 11? Are the others so cruel? You can't call them immature now?"

"The others simply assume that she doesn't talk to anybody. That is how it all started in the first place. She was too shy and did not speak to the other kids. The other kids mistook her attitude as being too haughty, I mean, nobody thought that shyness was her problem because she was so confident when talking to teachers and answering questions in class and all that. But she is just a really, really shy person. She cannot start a conversation with somebody who is not close to her.

"Then one day, some kid went along and asked why nobody talked to Radha and some other kid joked, 'She is too ugly; we can't talk to her!' And that fell in her ears.

"Back then she was alright with it, I mean, little children don't even know what is beautiful and what is ugly. But now, it is starting to pain her. Her confidence has diminished to zero, totally replaced by a monstrous inferiority complex. Oh God! It's scary."

"Haven't you tried convincing her? Tried telling her the true story? She would listen."

"I have told her and she has listened. And until sometime back she had no problem with it either. But now, all of a sudden she thinks it is all her problem. Every day she showers herself with self-depreciating harassment."

I was silenced. There was nothing I could do. Kanha would not listen, and Lakshmi was already trying her best. There was nothing I could do to help Radha. But at least I can help Kanha for the time being. I decided to help him prepare for his exams.

*"This can't go on like this! This is an invasion and it is ruining us, you have to do something to stop it!"*

*"You can see very clearly how things are going on out there. I am just an old fool – helpless old fool", said the frail voice of a weak brain in response to the concerns of several citizens of the body. Most of Kanha enjoyed the new regime, which actually provided from a lot of free-time, exercise, relaxation and the luxury of "comfort" - Music, dance, movies and all that.*

*"You cannot simply give up like this. You are our leader, our king! And now we are going to fight no matter what – for our leader", somewhat the same lines that the rebels spoke to Bahadur Shah Zafar, the last Mughal emperor before the revolt of 1857.*

*"You are our symbol, our inspiration and motivation. You have lead us for so many years, through a golden era! You have served us for so long. Now it is our turn to serve you. There is going to be mutiny! A coup! And you shall once again become our king!" The cells from different parts of his body, united by nothing but the sheer desire to get rid of their new master, pleaded to the brain and set out on their mission.*

*What to say, they were monumentally over-powered. The battle barely caused an itch on Kanha's scrotum, nothing more. What more can be possible when the a single cell is fighting against its own organ and the organ is supported by the rest of the body. Not just that the battle did not serve any purpose, it aggravated the damage as Kanha's penis took over complete control, not just suppressing but literally replacing the brain. And I stood there like a fool watching the events unfold.*

Again I failed, as the mid-term exams went down the drain for Kanha. That marked the beginning of a series of reversals for him. His notebook was incomplete, the assignments were never submitted, homework was not done and even his books were not brought to class. The only thing that remained of his performance was his regular attendance which did not change, for he wanted to be with his beautiful Chandrika, for as long as possible.

Within one month, 12 years of hard work and sincerity had been destroyed. The brutality with which his reputation was ruined crushed his parents, and all his previous teachers. News was very quick to fly that Kanha had become a spoilt child, it even reached the Principal's ears. Don't know whether he got mixed up in some bad friendship or if there was anything wrong in his home, his class teacher admitted to his mother, "But Kanha is behaving like a street rat in my class. I was told I received a gem, but this is too sad. Please do something about it."

And his parents too tried every weapon at their disposal, threats, emotional blackmail, love, advice and more emotional blackmail, but everything fell in his deaf ears. Not deaf exactly, full ears. Ears that refused to resonate anything except a very melodious, "Hi Kanha", from Chandrika's lips which he received once in a while.

Nothing more passed between the two. Kanha was too petrified to start a conversation with her and Chandrika had no intention of talking to a boy who ridiculously stalked her all the time. Courtesy alone made her say those "Hi Kanha". Courtesy, and an attempt to avoid the awkward scene he created all the time by foolishly staring at her.

Now, don't assume that Chandrika is the villain in this story. Actually she is a very, very nice girl, from what

I have seen of her. Very friendly, not a class topper but quite bright, very humble, which was a truly remarkable trait considering how beautiful she looked and very diplomatic, (especially when it comes to handling boys, for otherwise Kanha would have lost a couple of teeth by the end of class 11.)

On the other hand if you assume that Kanha was a jackass in behaving how he did… you are right. He was completely irrational, did things without purpose, without logic and without the barest sign of decency. For six long months this idiocy went on – music, movies, dance and endless ogling.

Then in the middle of the second term of school, a month after Onam, his English teacher presented him with his golden opportunity –Class assembly. Students were asked to come forward in a groups of 2-5 and put up a performance for the class that would last for 10-15 minutes. Miraculously (because, the way things were going, I was afraid Kanha would just end his life in the dreams of his beauty queen), Kanha summoned up his nerves and asked Chandrika to be his team-mate.

"An enactment of the English version of *Ramanan* by Changampuzha – what do you think?" Kanha proposed.

"Um…"

"Don't worry, I know the Malayalam version by heart and it won't take me much time to translate it. We will perform the scene where *Ramanan* herds his goats to the forest and Chandrika", he gestured her with a smile, "Asks him if she can accompany him. One of the best scenes in the poem, and quite simple to enact too. You just have to learn the dialogues."

"Aren't they really cheesy?"

"Artistic would be my word." Chandrika translated those words as, "Easy marks" and agreed. I was surprised that she did because even somebody like me, who finished school several decades back could predict how a classroom of 11th standard students would react to this:

*To herd goats in the forest, can I accompany you?*
*In the forest path, spring season must be blossoming*
*The trees must be full of flowers*
*Little love birds must be conducting a musical concert*
*To see all these sights, I too will join you!"*

Chandrika did sing these lines to her beloved Ramanan in front of 50 eleventh standard students who in-turn became hysterical. For Kanha however, who never cared for what his classmates thought that performance was a landmark on two counts.

Firstly, that was the only assignment he had completed on time during his higher secondary school. Secondly, that marked the beginning of a friendship between Chandrika and Kanha. Two magnificently superficial achievements!  Because the friendship that he thought was forged between them was nothing more than a 'Good Morning' in the morning and a 'Tata, bye-bye' after school. Kanha though, gave more credit to those exchanges and decided to build a relationship through that, or as they say in the movies – take it to the next level. "From level 0 to level 0.001", I told myself.

Shamelessly Kanha continued to pursue his dream. He added her on his Orkut friends list, got her phone number and went ahead with every opportunity to get in touch with her without the least thought of what she might think of him. Kanha had always been a person who thought only of himself – his obsession and his ambition, nothing else occupied his mind and this gave him a fatal weakness. He never knew what somebody else thought of him, and later in the story (like a few paragraphs later), this weakness will cause him agony.

Another six months went by, with Kanha making a lot of progress inside his head. Inside his head, meaning both, in his imaginary world and in terms of the schemes he had prepared to propose Chandrika and go forward in their relationship. By the end of 11th standard, which he managed to only scrape through, plans were ready till the birth of their second child and a fight was going on between the two if they wanted a third or not.

*Kanha: Heyy…*
*(Message sent at 7pm)*

*Kanha: How is it going?*
*(Message sent at 7.10pm)*

*Kanha: What are you doing right now?*
*Had dinner?*
*Any plans for the weekend?*
*(Message sent at 7.25pm)*

*Kanha: Hey, have you heard Om Shanthi Om songs? I just downloaded it. Simply Superbb!!! :D :D :D*
*(Message sent at 7.30pm)*

*Kanha: Then what else Chandrika? How's life? All well at home.*

*Kanha: And how is your exam preparation going on? Study well…*

*(Message sent at 7.35pm)*

*Kanha: You seem to be a little busy… Do reply soon…*
*(Message sent at 7.38pm)*

*Kanha: Heyy, wanted to ask you one more thing… Hope you don't mind…*
*(Message sent at 7.39pm)*

*Kanha: I am struggling with the Math's paper actually. Calculus, whoever invented it. Don't even feel like picking up the book. Do you think we can sit together and do a group study some time?"*
*(Message sent at 7.41pm)*

*Kanha: Are you watching TV now? Anything nice on… I am feeling bored!*
*(Message sent at 7.45pm)*

*Chandrika: Heyyy Kanha! ☺ ;-) sooooo sorry, I couldn't reply… I wasn't in front of the system actually. Yeah, the songs are really nice.*
*Kanha: Heyy…*
*Chandrika: Kanha, listen… really sorry but I have to hurry… Mom is calling me for dinner. See you tomorrow… And thanx for chatting! Bye!*
*(Message sent at 8.28pm)*

*Both Kanha and Chandrika were online from 7pm to 10pm. Neither was busy.*

The proposed date of proposal happened to be somewhere in the middle of their summer vacations, which would end rather quickly and extra classes for 12th standard would begin early. Till then, he planned to call her every day and make sure their friendship was strong. Chandrika, as a manner of courtesy did share some of her news with him and did not seem to be bored with his stories. But in a subtle manner she did make it clear that she had better things to do and avoided every point of contact that Kanha suggested.

"Hey, how about we go for a movie tonight?"

"Oh, sorry yaar. I am going to see my grandparents today."

"So how about one tomorrow?"

"Already made plans with Parvathy. She has been asking since the beginning of vacations"

"I have been too", Kanha said under his breath and continued with her, "Alright, so how about day after tomorrow?"

"Uhh… Oh yeah, sure! Which movie do you have in mind?"

"The new Mohanlal movie!" He said bouncing with excitement and not feeling shy to show the joy in his voice.

"Ohhh… that one. I already saw it man. Hey, my mom is calling, gotta go! Bye", and that's how you press a nail on a balloon of excitement.

But Kanha took every word to his heart, a heart that pumped optimism and blood in equal quantities and decided to propose her to be his girlfriend, just as he had planned.

That morning he woke up before the sun and was clean and ready at his breakfast table, just as he was, once upon a time, on a regular basis, long, long ago. The "Mother Look" appeared on Archana's face, mixed with a smile of hopeful change in her son. No words were exchanged between the family and Kanha locked himself in his room immediately after breakfast to choose his attire for the special date. In five minutes he made his decision to wear a plain blue shirt with black pants, that, as he was not aware of, happened to be in fashion during the mid-nineties. Dressed up, hair combed and body perfumed, he sat at his table with one pen and two sheets of paper that he had torn from his Maths notebook, which had a lot of blank pages here and there… and everywhere. One, for the love letter he wanted to give and for the proposal speech.

"Chandrika", the finalized version of his speech went something like this, "we have been very good friends for around an year now and know each other very well. And what I know about you is that you are the smartest, brightest and most beautiful girl I have ever seen, and I am sure that I will never see anyone nicer or sweeter than you in my life. Chandrika, I promise that I will be just the man you want, the guy who takes care of you like a princess and is there for everything that you will ever need, that you will ever want. My sweetheart, will you be my girlfriend?"

He practiced it a couple of times in front of the mirror and was happy with the way it sounded. He was really pleased and I wanted to puke, especially at his remark of the nicest girl.

He lifted his pen to write the letter but excitement made him uncontrollably restless and he rushed to grab his phone and call her up.

"Hello? Chandrika, can we meet today?" Kanha was panting.

"Oh, Kanha, hey, hi. Today, oh sorry dude, I –"

"No buts no sorry's, please! This is really important, you have to make it"

"Today is impossible Kanha I have a date with Aravind", Chandrika blurted out. The words date and Aravind went like bullets into his head.

"WHAT!?" Kanha shouted.

"Well", Chandrika continued shyly with a giggle, "He proposed to me today morning. And… you know… hey will catch you later da", Chandrika cut the phone and Kanha was paralysed.

I thought Kanha reached rock bottom when he got 76% for his final exams in 11th. But the freefall was not going to stop. Oh! Did I say that he 'managed to scrape through 11th standard'? Hey, don't look at me like that, I am a nerd's conscience and I had been with a nerd for a really long time. A fall from 94-91 is itself a national disaster for our kind. Reaching 70s is apocalypse!

But 12th standard began with a series of events that continued throughout the year until Kanha touched 59% in his pre-board exams and he was left facing the boards with no notes to study, no concept that he remembered and absolutely nobody to help him out. This is how it all happened, starting … With Kanha being slowly pulled out his heart-break. For a couple of days his digestive system wouldn't work because of the shock and his heart alternated between high blood pressure and low blood pressure. His respiratory system contributed with breathlessness, but that was mainly because of the tearless crying that Kanha did. And to be frank with all of you, as Kanha's one and only conscience, I have to admit that what he had for her was not true love. But the hopes and expectations of having such a beautiful girl as his girlfriend, the thought of putting his arm around and watching a movie together, the idea of her resting on his lap, of them walking hand in hand around the school, when all that was crushed all of a sudden – that was heartbreaking!

And like every other un-genuine heartbreak, Kanha could recover quickly, not back to normal however. Back to his thoughts of Chandrika, and, as a new twist, his plans for a revenge to Aravind. A triangular World War I began inside his head, with myself and the old Kanha (bits and pieces of him), and a formidable new Kanha:

"You are no idiot to put all this hard-work and just simply stare at the world when somebody else steals your girl. Chandrika is yours Kanha, all yours, and you HAVE to win her back. And you can't leave Aravind alone either. He has asked for it."

"Hard-work indeed", that was me, "Listening to junk music and watching movies all night was indeed hard-work. Kanha, snap out of it, this isn't the real you. You know how much you have really worked hard. For your ambitions!"

"Laughable ambitions. Ambitions that you are shy to speak of even in your mind. Schemes, childish, such childish thoughts. Stupid thoughts. And to think that your conscience would encourage them." Hey did he just say conscience? Kanha didn't recognize me as his conscience, no human can. Oh, figure of speech maybe.

"Nobody can judge who the real you is Kanha, except yourself. Don't condemn yourself as a stupid nerd with idiotic plans to save the world. You are more than that, you are a man. A real practical man, with practical thoughts and tangible issues."

"Revenge isn't a tangible issue. Throw the thought out of your mind, it is irrational."

"It is the universal truth. Balance… he has given you pain and you ought to give it back to him. I am not asking you to hurt him out of volition. Just repay what he has given you."

"Not with more pain"

"With exactly the right amount of pain."

"Kanha, you worshipped Mahatma Gandhi and his ideals. You know better."

"You are the only person in the world who reads about Mahatma Gandhi. Kanha, snap out of it and look around you. How many Gandhians do you see? How many people practice non-violence and all that? Now do you think all of them are fools. They are all smart people Kanha, and all of them have had the same battle in their heads and all of them have chosen what is right. What is the best for them"

"Something doesn't become right simply because everybody chooses it."

"A nerd always believes that he is only person with brains. You have to understand, everybody is smart. Everybody has brains and uses it and going with a majority opinion is always, if you ask me, the right choice."

"You can't hate for love"

"So? Revenge it is"

Had he used these skills a few months earlier, he would have aced the debate contest. I here, am a conscience with 15 years of experience in guiding a human, and 50 years of experience in bringing up children (during my human life), and this fellow easily outclassed me with his arguments. I am not admitting that he was right, simply saying that he raised a bunch of good points and more importantly, said them well. Kanha was thoroughly convinced and got set to plan his revenge. His body however had some reservations about the decision.

*I could feel it creep into the back of Kanha's head the day Chandrika hung up on him. An eerie presence. Something disturbing… but could not point a finger. A gut feeling that something was not right, something out of the ordinary, but what?*

*There seemed to be some kind of wall between me and Kanha. His organs became silent all of a sudden. They don't talk to each other, they don't respond to me. I was being ignored, my existence was barely acknowledged, I felt isolated… helpless.*

"Everybody knows Rajesh and Aravind are enemies to the core. So if you want to attack Aravind, you have to befriend Rajesh. Get into their gang, and the ideas to execute your vengeance will follow."

"Rajesh and Aravind are students!" I had little hope of convincing him, Kanha wasn't even listening to me. But I said, "sometimes they fight, sometimes they argue and sometimes they tear each other apart, but none of that is real Kanha don't believe it. You will get into Rajesh's gang and within a month or two Rajesh and Aravind will become best friends, and you will end up earning both their ire. So far nobody has hurt you in school Kanha, but trust me if you go nosing into their business and try to create any trouble – they will strike at you."

My prediction was spot on, and everything I said happened word by word, But for Kanha, there was more in store.

During his period of fanatic studies he had earned a bunch of enemies. Not enemies exactly, but students who despised him. Not just that he wouldn't help them out in studies but managed his best to create troubles for them by asking for tests and submitting his home-works well in advance. Something that was not so easy for most of the other kids in class to cope up with. Some of them suffered dearly because of this approach of Kanha and some of their conscience talked to me too about this. They told me that Kanha was making the class go too fast and some students felt genuinely left behind. Students who had other interests, in sports or music, had to sacrifice a lot.

What a co-incidence! Among those students who hated Kanha, a dozen of them (the worst hit lot) had actually planned to kill him (I can't thank their conscience enough). And after 10th standard, this lot had joined hands to form Rajesh's gang.

"Hey guys, how's life?" I remember Kanha walking up to Rajesh while he was in a cocoon created by his friends, the ones I just talked to you about.

"Heyyyy….. Kanhaaa…. What a pleasant surprise? What the fuck do you want?" Ajay asked.

"Nothing. I was just..." He didn't say anything, but made his purpose very clear. He wanted to be friends with them. And the gang took him in with open arms and a warm welcome. What better way to cast their revenge.

It began with obnoxious bullying and ragging (which was to grow to notorious levels). Slowly, through constant nagging, they found out the purpose of his friendship and his huge crush for Chandrika. "We are there for you man", Achuth promised on behalf of the group.

They taught him to ride a bike. Was that to impress girls or just because they wanted somebody to get caught for not having a license - is not a mystery for me. They took him to watch porno, and its ramifications in Kanha's body was a nightmare. He bunked classes with them and smuggled cell phones for them.

"Wanna have a drink", Govind asked him with a sly smile once. I dashed to meet Rajesh's conscience and begged him to convince Rajesh and veto the decision. The conscience – Dinesh, agreed and talked to his human. He was a fellow with a very mischievous flair, but he listened to his conscience (hence his good marks and leadership abilities), and obeyed him selectively (hence the drinking).

"Can't take it too far with him. No need."

"Sorry bro, probably next time", Govind consoled Kanha. Kanha needed consolation.

In the last day of school, even teachers shed their professionalism to say good-byes to their children. They too were among friends. The clerks, peons, cleaners and office staff too waved their hands, some shed a tear as they bid farewell to students who had irritated or nagged or annoyed them since they were 4. To see the children grow a beard and walk out of school, the emotion was overwhelming.

The school corridors, the banyan tree that stood outside, the huge football ground, black-board, chalk box, dusters, the fearful staff-room, all of it seemed to come to life and give you a hug. And none of the students wanted to let go. Boys and girls, eyes and cheeks, wet and salty, slowly stepped out of the building.

And the most treasured friends? They promised never to let go. To always guard the other's back. Gangs that had names shouted for their slogans, lifting each other on their shoulder. And when the nostalgia became violent, shirt pockets were torn and sometimes the whole shirt was torn. "Thanks a lot yaar", the victim would say and give his friends a hug. Invariably tear his shirt too.

Rajesh too said good-bye to Aravind. Aravind gave him a fist punch and the rival gangs said emotional farewells.

Radha too was merry with a little group of 4 girls that cried on each other's shoulder.

Kanha walked out of the school campus silently. Nobody talked to him. He talked to nobody either. "Bah, Humbug!"

Classes had finally got over. The pre-board exams would be conducted in January followed by a month's exam leave and school life will be officially concluded after the Board Exams in March.

But Kanha had no intention to study. And the three of us (his parents and I) had no intention of giving up on him. "I know everything. I can handle it" he said and reclined in his room wondering what to do. A bunch of porn was downloaded. He tried to get in touch with his Rajesh gang but none of them responded. He wanted to watch T.V. but his mother had refused to allow him. That took her a ton of will power, as Archana had never said No to her son. So Kanha was forced to sit in his room and pretend to study. Very often film magazines happened to slip out of his books.

The pre-boards too got over and Kanha scored a magnificent 59%. Disappointment had turned to hopelessness for his teachers. His parents prayed that it did not go further down in his boards. Trying to convince him over and over again had exhausted me. Every word I said fell to deaf ears.

*Click* Idea! I had read in one of the books, in one of the hundreds of books I had browsed to find a cure for this hooliganism that Kanha was behaving with. Hey, what did you guys think, I was just sitting there and enjoying the show? One of the books pointed out a basic principle that humans listen to their conscience when they have nothing else to do. And that is the best opportunity to convince a human.

Kanha sat on his chair doing absolutely nothing. Even his mind seemed to be blank, devoid of thoughts. That was supposed to be a golden opportunity for me, my voice was supposed to pierce into his head. But he couldn't hear a word. Something happened to be truly fishy. A wall between myself and Kanha was there. I still couldn't figure out what it was. What could it be?

I went back to the beginning – since his birth. I admit that Kanha was never an ordinary child and his character was never, what one might say, normal. His behaviour, his attitude, his style, his likes and dislikes, they were all different.

Kanha was least interested in sports or fashion. He wasn't tech-savvy and did not have a taste for video games. Movies too were not on his wish list throughout his childhood. He was a very disciplined child till 10th standard. Along the way he picked up an ambition, or rather he cultivated it throughout his childhood, an ambition to save the world. But that never affected his character.

Then in 11th standard, everything changed. But the change was not ultra-wires... (Wow! I have been hanging out with too many Chartered Accountants. Yeah, most of the humans I guide, after Kanha that is, happen to be CAs. Hence the legal term), the changes in him were not inconsistent with his core character. His obsession with obedience had changed to an obsession for a girl. And of course, the political shift of power in his body too was a reason. Everything till there was logical.

Then, in class 12, he planned a revenge. The arguments he put up against me... right now when I look back, they seem to be oddly out of place. Out of character. As if, somebody else was trying to convince him. Dual personality? Nahh. Spirit entering his body? Nahh. He was still the same person but... his character suffered a radical change.

"Sir?" I asked my manager right away, "I have never read about it. But is there something called an anti-conscience?"

"A what?"

"Anti-conscience sir. An evil conscience, who instead of guiding you, tries to make you go the wrong way?"

"Dev, you have been in this business for quite a while now and you must be very thorough with the basics by now. You very well know that only those with a pure heart are permitted to enter afterlife."

"Yes I know that sir. But I can find no logical explanation to what is going on with Kanha over here. His mind is blank but I still am not being able to talk to him. As if, somebody is blocking my voice. As if, somebody else is trying to act as his conscience. Like… a wall"

With a *POP* my manager appeared before me. The man who always wore a laugh on his face, someone whom I feared would say, "What is Rahul Dravid, the wall, doing here?" was tense, tangibly tensed. He would have been sweating like a pig, even wet his pants, if he were human, so looked his face.

"Where is he?" my manager asked and I led him to Kanha. "Stay right here", he said went got sucked into Kanha's head. "ARGHHHH!!!!", Kanha grabbed his throbbing head and started screaming. I entered his head too.

Kanha's brain had become a battle field for two bright flashes of light. My manager and another soul – Aha! I was right, there is an anti-conscience! The two of them were fighting it out in Kanha's head, and the brain seemed to heat up. I wanted to grab them both and throw them out, but they were flying around at the speed of light, or so it looked. So instead I tried consoling the brain, "Come on, you can do it! You can handle the pain! Yes, you can do it! Keep it cool." And in return the brain was swearing at me.

The fight reached a fever high and it seemed his brain would bleed if it continued, so I communicated the message to my manager and soon, like within 30 seconds or so, both flashes of light *popped* out of the scene. And Kanha sat at his chair with a feeling as if a giant boulder was taken off his head.

# Chapter 3

# Resilience

"The monster has been inside his body for around an year and only now you inform me!?" Praveen (that was my manager's name) shouted at me angrily.

"I didn't know... how would I know?"

"You must have noticed abnormalities. You should have reported to me immediately"

"I did notice abnormalities but I thought I could handle it. I didn't know it was something so severe, nobody warned me. I did refer tons of books... What was that anyway?"

Praveen answered with a sigh, "You can call it an anti-conscience if you want. The idea is the same. A very, very rare case, not even one in a billion."

But there is not supposed to be any evil in afterlife...

"There is always an exception. Anyways, you needn't bother yourself with all this stuff, I will handle it. Get back to work now", Praveen said and hurried off. Such a busy fellow, always in a hurry. That is another one of the reasons I didn't contact him when I noticed the abnormality.

I got back home quickly and saw Kanha in shreds. He was completely lost, his head throbbing like never before, his body sweating with panic. I understood that he was slowly recovering from the kind of trance that was going on and only then understood the horror of what had happened.

"Relax, it's alright", I tried to console him but his worries were different. He was concerned not of his messed up past, but of the terrifying and imminent Board Exams. In a stuttering voice with tearful eyes Kanha asked, "What am I going to do?"

He had no notes to prepare, no memory of what was taught in class and no basic subject knowledge, so even if he wanted to start studying from scratch it would be impossible. For the practical subjects like Accountancy and Mathematics, he had no idea about the underlying concepts. The other theory subjects, there was tons to memorize, with exams just a month away. And this time, Kanha would not be content with 50s or 60s. As a matter of fact, nothing less than 95% (at least) would stop a heart attack. The old Kanha was back, and clueless. Now it is my task to put him back on track.

"Kanha, listen to me", I knew that wouldn't work, so I went with, "KANHA! YOU ARE GOING TO OBEY ME NOW!" My voice echoed in his head like a thunderstorm and he sat up to it. Now that I have your attention, "We are going to work it out and you will get the marks that you want. Don't worry about it!"

"But that is impossible!" Kanha cried. "It is just IMPOSSIBLE. I have to study two years syllabus in one month. There is no time to study or even go through. Preparing for exams is out of the question… I…"

"JUST SHUT UP AND SIT BACK", so obnoxious! You calm your voice for one second and they start to fight back. "You have had it your way all along and got yourself in this mess. NOW YOU LISTEN TO ME!" I SHOUTED! I mean, I shouted. And that did seem to have the desired impact.

"Sit there calm yourself down, that is the first thing you have to do. Take deep breaths and CALM DOWN", the way is said it, I admit, was ironic. But that would do.

As Kanha tried to relax himself I entered his body which was the pinnacle of chaos. Nobody knew what was going on. I stepped up and took command.

Very quickly I informed the body of what was going on, about Kanha's regret of not being able to prepare, of the lack of time and other difficulties they faced. Political heat was brewing up inside as all the cells began to turn against the testicles, who after all, were the ones who started all the problems. "We have bigger problems to solve right now. Kanha is in trouble, our Kanha!" I shouted, managing to grab their attention.

"There are internal issues I agree and many of you are not satisfied with the way things are going. I know all that."

"The brain is responsible for all this. The brain is not doing its job properly." The stomach shouted.

"I have always done my job right. As long as I had support I have done my job right. The limbs were too adamant that I give in to the demands of the penis."

"That is because we were never given our due respect. We never got what we deserved and we still continue to protest. As long as Kanha has this attitude towards his muscular system we will not conform with his needs"

"The limbs are right", the lungs added. "He barely goes out. We need more oxygenated air."

"You can say that", the skin cells retorted. "We are the ones to get torn apart. And all sun makes us go dark. The price is too high. We cannot afford to meet the demands of the lungs. You can sit there in the comfort of your ribs – safe and happy."

"Don't go whining about pain", the limbs interceded. "We suffer more pain than you do when he gets hurt. There is a risk, we all know, but it is quintessential for his health."

"There is no oxygen outside. It's all dust and pollution", the nose pointed out to the lungs.

"I am not asking him to walk on the road in the middle of the traffic. There are so many parks-"

"ENOUGH!" Ughh... seriously, some politicians can be so irritating! One eventually has to tell them all, no matter how adamant they are, no matter how powerful they are, no matter how unchangable they are – one has to command, "ENOUGH!". One has to change things; not just transpose the way they are. Today the skin is happy and muscles are upset, tomorrow the muscles are happy and the skin is upset. Go on with this cyclical process for a while and when you get tired of it, try something entirely different. Invite a whole new ruler who has no idea what he is doing. And when you try to get rid of the new guy and clear up the mess he has made, the old issues crop up again. Muscles or Skin?

"The nation has not done justice to its people", I said to the cells. "And there are a bunch of issues to be rectified. Many of you are upset, many of you have been upset since Kanha's birth, I know. But if things continue to be the way they are, everybody will have to suffer!"

"Let them", the limbs shouted. "Why should we suffer alone? Let them suffer with us!"

"YOU FOOLS! YOU HAVE AN OPPORTUNITY TO MAKE YOURSELVES HEARD AND YOU USE TO CAST YOUR REVENGE?" The limbs were silenced and I continue. "This is the opportunity to understand that we are one. We are one body, connected to each other in more than a million ways. Nobody can suffer alone, and this is the time that we finally understand that. Haven't we learnt our lesson, if one of us is in pain, then we all end up in pain. We have just seen that and learnt it. Sadly, we had to do that the hard way.

"Now is the time that we get united and turn a fresh page. We have an enemy out there; a crisis is brewing up and we need to fight it. A war is going to begin my friends and we have to fight it not as limbs and skin and stomach but as one body. This is the time for you to understand your purpose. We have to fight for Kanha!"

There was a buzz among many of the cells (just like the one you see in most of the movies after this kind of speech). I turned to the brain and said, "What do you have to say about this?"

"Say what?"

"Exercise. What do you think about it?"

"I…"

"You have been an outstanding leader and you will continue to be one. I am with you, Kanha's family is with you. But the rest of the body, you have to bring them to your side and that is possible now only if you give them a genuine promise. And only if you take a vow that you will fight for their rights. That you will actually behave like a true leader. Can you do that? For Kanha, can you lead the war?"

"A war?"

"One month, five subjects, five exams, five hundred marks – and our stakes are too high. What is going to happen in the coming month is a war. A Serious War. And I know you can win it, you have proven yourself too many times. Will you do it?"

"I will. I will do it. For Kanha and for all of us", the brain told me and addressed the other cells in his body through his neurons, demanding their rapt attention as he did during every exam that Kanha faced, "We have been through 2 years of hell and we are tired of it. We need to change. We need to be what we used to be. No! We need to be better than that. I have commanded you and lead you many a times. This time, I am asking you, to fight with me. As equals. Can we fight?"

Was it nostalgia or was it just that his speech was rather good, but there was a change in attitude all of a sudden. The brain's old supporters cheered for him in full vigour and the others too joined in. Hope was fuelled throughout the body and the limbs too were touched. "I promise", the brain added, "things will be better for you from now on. And as for you", it told the testicles, "We will work things out with you too", and that totally won their support too. The body had been united, and the battle field was ready.

Kanha could feel the change, the positivity flowing in his veins, the muscles getting energized and his brain was electrified. I stood by them and saw them

sort out the obstacles one by one. The very first one –
"From where will I arrange notes to study?"

"Ask Radha", I told Kanha before his brain could
suggest anything.

"She is science. How can she help me?" Was it the
brain or the soul? One of them asked.

"She is your only friend."

"I know", it stung him a little to admit that. "But she
has no other friends either. How will she help me in
commerce?"

"All the teachers like her. She can arrange notes
and all the material you will require to face the exams."

"I haven't talked to her in ages."

"It is time you finally talk to her." I knew it shouldn't
be the first thing on my mind but if their friendship is
re-ignited, that would be another wonderful success.
And apparently I had convinced Kanha.

Right away he got dressed up and headed to
Radha's house. "Tell your mother what you are upto?"
I told him.

"Amma, I am going to a friend's house to collect
some notes. Have to start studying, will be back in half
an hour". That brought a smile to her face. Even if the
exams don't go as expected there are going to be a lot
of collateral benefits. And I seem to be doing a pretty
decent job.

*Knock*Knock* Radha opened the door and
greeted Kanha with a dumbstruck expression. "Long
time!" Kanha waved his hand stupidly. Suddenly he
noticed the little feather lying on her head and brushed
it away. "Still don't bath do you?" he joked. "What are
you doing here?" Radha asked and Kanha was about

to ask for help just when I told him, "Apologize first." And he did.

*Dear Diary,*

*Or should I start calling you dearest diary? No, not because you are the only one who gives me company. Because I am so full of love for everything around me. I love my life, the people around me, the things I do, the dreams I have – I feel so blessed.*

*Today again I spoke to Reshma and Shreya for around an hour. Amma did say that I shouldn't be spending so much time on phone but relationships are simply more important than anything else in the world. I feel that "people" should be first on every person's priority list. What you give a person is truly the best investment one can make in the world. The most beautiful investment. And the best part is that you are guaranteed of return. What you sow, so you reap. Call me selfish because I am, because I know that I will receive everything I have given with interest… some day. And hence, now when you can, give as much love as possible. Yes, selfish reasons, I know. But whatever, go ahead, go and love as much as possible. Give as much as possible.*

*And the feeling is truly special. The satisfaction you get when you have made some person happy. When you see a smile on some person's face. When you a rub a tear off somebody's cheek. When you give a shoulder to somebody, a hand of support, a word of kindness… It can change the world, I know it! And it is such a simple thing to do. Just love!*

*The fact that there are so many millions deprived in the world. Food, clothing, shelter – men and women who have none of it. Children who will never know the taste of any of it!*

*It is sad... It has to change. God has given me so much! So close friends, every luxury a girl could hope for. Good education, loving parents, amazing teachers, a beautiful school, so many opportunities... I can reach the sky and not because I have put any effort. But because almighty has gifted it to me, every fortune I have cherished in life so far and everything that I am God will give me in the future.*

*Now, it is up to me to give it back to the world. Give a lot of happiness, give people everything that I have received. That is my ambition. That is my purpose in life. A billion smiles! I can do that – I am positive. With a little arrogance let me say," When Radha is around, how can somebody wear a frown."*

- Read Radha's diary, the day before Kanha met her again, after a very long time.

And Radha was Radha. The notes and guides and IIT-JEE material were spread on the table accompanied by a couple of pens and pencils which proved that she was busy at work, but that didn't stop her from ringing a few teacher who had not taught her and beg them to provide the notes they had. They readily agreed to her request.

Radha accompanied Kanha to their school, where she met all the teachers, collected the notes, guides and sample question papers for preparation. "Thanks a billion Radha!" Kanha said.

"Anytime Kanha. Hey, I gotta go. Lots to study."

"JEE huh? How is it?"

"Let's wait and see." She said and hurried off.

"Hey Radha", Kanha stopped her and added, and that made me proud, "Thank you so much. Owe you for life!"

Radha turned around, so gracefully... so beautifully... "I am always there for you my brother!"

*One word can change the world!*

And Kanha headed home too. It did take him a little more than half an hour and his mother was starting to suspect whether he had wandered off for some hooliganism, but to see him back with a ton of books made her proud.

Problem number two – How to study all of this stuff in one month.

The brain took command and prepared a time table right away. "We have four weeks with us and five subjects to study. English will be easy to handle and we can study that lessons whenever we get bored. So that makes it four subjects to handle. One week we will need to revise with all these guides and sample question papers, and I guess we need a week's time to get started with all the subjects. So two weeks and four subjects. Piece of cake.

"In the first week we will have a first reading of all the notebooks and textbooks we have. That will give us an idea of what we are facing, what is our strong area, what is our weakness and how to apportion the remaining two weeks for the four subjects. That is how we get started. So Kanha, let's get started!"

The huge books were picked up, notes first and read through. And the body stood together as one unit to get him through the literary sleeping pills namely business studies and economics. Eyes were alert, ears turned off, bladder in very good control and his digestive system reminding him in a very disciplined manner, only three times a day, that it was time to eat. Sleep was a major obstacle and the brain did its best to stay late into the night and wake up before the sun shines. His muscles were always energetic and his testicles did a very good job by sitting there very, very silently.

Week one went by as per schedule and so did week two and week three. Week four however gave him a nightmare. As he picked up the question papers one by one, his brain seemed to shut down. The adrenaline gland burst open and the entire body seemed to be in red alert.

"Calm down, calm down!" I said.

"This is ridiculous. I just spent three sleepless nights studying every single thing in the notebook and also covered the textbooks. Why can't I answer these questions?" Kanha had freaked out.

I was about to reply but his brain was ready with an answer, "We have just had one learning and that too in a hurry. We are not yet ready to answer question. Let's do one things, take up the guides and answer them one by one. That will make one round of revision for us. We will postpone the sample question papers for the day before exams. And we will do one final round of revision on that day too."

Tackling the humungous guides was much harder than anyone imagined and demanded, way too much time and energy. "This is not practically possible. We have to find another way out!" One portion of his brain suggested.

"We will go as per weightage. Let's refer the portions that are most important in the examination point of view and then we will take up the other questions. We may not be able to cover the entire book but we can try to finish off a good majority. And the other minor portions, we will see to that in our final revision."

Archana and Hari were there too, right by Kanha to help him out. Giving him company at late nights, waking him up if him over-slept, preparing the perfect meals to keep him going through the day and taking care of all the chores that he was required to do as a big boy. And occasionally they called him out of his room for some television show and the brain welcomed his mother's invite which gave it much needed rest. Archana would also make sure that Kanha's exhaustion didn't let him cozy up with the television and asked him to return after 15-30 minutes. That was rarely required but when the brain lacked will-power, mother-power was there to the rescue and Kanha would get back to work.

The real job began two days before the exams. As the reality of exams became almost tangible, so did his fear of a very possible disaster. He was sure that his marks wouldn't be so bad and there was certain to be a significant improvement from his pre-board exams, getting 95% was a contingent matter. His brain was not able to perform to its best, as the fear began to consume a lot of energy.

"Don't worry. Let me see if I can handle it", and the heart put a remarkably strong fight to keep itself calm and steady.

Exam No. 1 – cracked!

Kanha did it with the grace that he had maintained throughout childhood. Very carefully he had read the entire question paper and as the answer sheet fell on his table, the answers flowed out of his pen. 100 marks were equally divided into 180 minutes and the paper was handed over to the invigilator only after a round of checking. And with one exam down, the burden of fear was taken out of his brain. Exams 2, 3 and 4 were just a cakewalk.

He had four days to prepare for his last exam – Mathematics. Taking into account these four days, Kanha has given least preference to Maths in his study schedule. He was right in doing so too, as four days was sufficient time to do enough and more number of problems from his guide and the sample question papers. But on the very first day, Kanha woke up late, the wings of his ceiling fan sending an abnormal chill through his body. He tightly covered his body with the blanket, but could feel no warmth. At the breakfast table his mother placed her palm on his forehead and announced with a shriek – "You have fever!"

The entire body was dysfunctional for the day. His head throbbed with pain and did nothing else. His mouth was tasteless and his nose was running wildly. His skin was heating up like wildfire Kanha could feel pain in his muscles too. That day itself he visited the doctor who recommended a day of bed rest and anti-biotic.

The immune system was hard at work and literally at war. The anti-biotic did its job by giving much needed support to the immunity system and by the end of day two, the fever had subsided, leaving two days to face the much dreaded Mathematics exam.

"Sleepless nights!" That was the solution suggested by the brain for the problem that his body faced. "You all have given me great support for the past two months. You all have been through a lot of pain, I know that. For another two more days I ask for your support. If we go through two sleepless nights, then we can easily crack the exams, and after that we will have plenty of time to take rest. All of us can relax and celebrate. Till then, we need this!"

The entire body gave its assent for the adventure and Kanha stayed up for 48 hours and completed his preparations. There was no thought of sleep in Kanha's head and even when the problems began to bore Kanha, we pulled up all his will power to go ahead with his study schedule. One by one he completed all the chapters and one round of revision. Tirelessly he worked his way through the most complicated problems, exercising his brain to its limits and solving every problem he came across, some by himself, and some with the assistance of a manual. And after 48 hours, Kanha was fully prepared to face the question paper. But everyone overlooked one minor flaw in the plan. Two sleepless nights gave Kanha no energy to write the exams. He realized that only when his eyes began to give in as the question paper was placed on his table.

"Don't sleep now. Don't sleep now, just three more hours to go!" But one by one, his organs began to fail. His fingers couldn't move, his eyes couldn't stay open, his brain wouldn't think, his spine could not stay upright.

The table in front of his was somehow pulling his head towards it.

"KANHA! WAKE UP!" I shouted at him and he jerked awake. "Three more hours. Just pull yourself together. Please!"

With horror Kanha saw the brand new mess he had brought himself into. "I can do it. Just three more hours." He tried to pull himself but even the brains wasn't there to listen. Tenderly he picked up the question paper and read it, but it made no sense to him. He could somehow read the words and figures but could not understand them. "Wake up you stupid brain!" Kanha and I shouted together and the brain reacted with a faded spark. "Come on, come on... WAKE UP!"

The brain just didn't listen to me. Finally, Kanha took the ultimate whip of his will power and pulled it awake. "I don't know if I will kill myself, but you are going to be with me for another 3 hours!" With a stretch of hands, a wild yawn and crock of knuckles, Kanha picked up his question paper one more time and read it through. After every question his brain would turn off and Kanha would shake his head a couple of times until it was back on.

Every five minutes he asked for a glass of water, drank half of it, and carefully, making sure none of it fell on his answer paper, splashed the rest of it on his face. The answers were slow to come and each question took more time than he normally would have. But his fingers were fast and writing his thoughts down didn't cause him so much trouble. "Thanks", the brain whispered to the muscles of his fingers and continued to work.

And like a very typical cinema climax, that exam too got over, with Kanha managing to answer every question, quite rightly. While in normal movies you have the hero struggling against his pain and fatal injuries to save the world, in this story, the hero struggles against his sleep to write his 12th standard board exams.

I feel it was a commendable job that he did. The mess was something that he brought onto himself, but he did get through it, and I salute that. The 12th standard boys achievement may not save the world, but he did his part. And isn't that the most important thing?

Like a very good boy, Kanha said 'Hi' to Radha when he saw her and told her a billion thanks. She smiled, he smiled back and rubbed the feather off her head. As Kanha entered his house, Praveen pulled me back to his room. That surprised me for a second, but I knew that was about to happen any second. My tenure as Kanha's conscience was finally over.

"What will happen to him now?" I asked my manager.... I mean, Praveen.

"You can always see that. Arun is going to be his next conscience. He will keep you updated if you want. But till then, you have another task."

I thanked him and took up the file of my next assignment. He was a chartered accountant, a really angry man who ran a successful practice. "Easy job. Just have a check on his anger. And this is his first human life. Try to make sure it's his last too."

On my way to the library, where Praveen asked me to read through the entire file, I met Arun and told him, in a very emotional dialogue. "Take good care of Kanha. He is a great guy!". Arun nodded.

The new file was in my hand, but thoughts were elsewhere. I wanted to know what Kanha was doing at that moment. Did he get a good sleep? Did he go to the park for a jog? Did he talk to Radha after that? His CPT exams for CA were due in a couple of months. Did he start preparing for that?

I was with him for nearly every second in his life and being away from him was truly painful. "I will be back for you", I promised myself and took up my next task.

# Book II

# *Chapter 4*

# *Paradise*

Sita woke up when the moon was still full in the sky. She moved the curtains of her house and looked at the billions of twinkling dots that accompanied the cool and radiant celestial miracle. A gentle breeze touched her face and woke her smile up too. Quickly she stood up and rushed to the kitchen.

"Where is Laxman Appa?"

"Didn't see him yesterday night also. You can go alone today", her father spoke from the centre of a splendour that always mesmerised her. All the vegetables and fruits were peeled, cut, chopped or grilled as the dish demanded and placed on various plates around him so artistically that one would wonder whether he was cooking or decorating the kitchen. Sita decided that she had to be back before the firewood was ignited, because when he actually began cooking, the aroma would take her to another world.

It did every day. A different world every day. And when you finally kissed the food, it would put you in a trance from which you could recover only an hour after the plate was licked clean. The entire village was blessed with that fortune three times a day, and it never got old.

Sita placed a kiss on her father's bearded cheek and rushed outside to have a bath in the river. The sun wouldn't be up for another couple of hours but she preferred her swim in the river before anyone else did. For that was when the water was coolest and her swim will be accompanied only by the ripples she would make. That was the only hour when the forest would speak in whispers.

She stepped out of her brick house and walked through the narrow path behind her house, fenced by tall grass and other plants which she never learnt the names of. Sita thought of her friend Malati who has walked with her through the same path countless times, announcing the name of each plant that touched them and sing about its beauty. Not a song that rhymed, not a song that timed, but one that pleased the ears and was fun to recite.

"This one has really huge leaves that are shaped like a cup. And leaf is not an ordinary one – it doesn't allow water to flow away."

"This flower changes colours from red during the day to blue during the night."

"This tree bears the sweetest fruit – Mambazham fruit."

And every word she said was true. Sita knew that because even her father agreed that the tree Malati pointed out did bear the sweetest fruit, so sweet that you could crush one fruit to mix it with rice to feed more than 50 people. "53 plates of rice to be precise", Sita's father said.

The walk slowly turned into a flip, Sita easily dodged the roots of huge trees that protruded from the path and tripped anyone who walked the path even in broad daylight. But Sita never fell, was that because she knew each sand on the ground or because no stone on the ground would dare to hurt their wonderful girl.

The path ended at the bank of a huge river that was a mother to all the five villages that made their home. It fed the astounding flora and fauna that lived in the surrounding forest and villages that lived with the forest. Everybody, the trees, plants, animals, birds and even the people were content and nobody slept in an empty stomach. And as long as Drupa, Sita's father was in the kitchen, they slept with a full heart too.

Sita stepped down the bank of the river undressed herself and dived into the freezing water that brought goose bumps all over her body. And she loved it! She pushed into the depths of the river, swam back up and like a pendulum she swam till the middle of the river. The water was still all around her, even the ripples she made had disappeared and not a leaf moved in the forest that curtained their river on either side. Sita swam in a circular path to reach where she had started.

As she swam through the depths of the mother river, a hand reach for her legs and pulled her out. "Are you late today?" Laxman, Sita's brother, elder to her by two years, asked.

"No, just as usual. You are too early it seems."

"Maybe. I have been swimming for more than an hour, waiting for you"

"Where were you yesterday?"

"Was giving company to Das as he gazed at the stars all night." Das was Malati's counterpart. If Malati knew everything about plants, Das knew everything about the sky. Malati was Sita's best friend and Das was Laxman's best friend. And a really impressive fellow he was indeed.

There were many who could draw pictures, some drew on sand, some painted on rocks, but Das was the only one who could draw pictures in the sky. He used the sky as his canvas and the stars made up his pictures. He drew a bear, a lion, a bird and so many other things with the stars in the sky and every person in the village was hypnotised by his skill. Everyone was indeed in love with him and apparently he did put a lot of effort to earn the fanfaronade.

"At first he only drew pictures but now he has started noticing how those pictures move every night. Do you remember that he had drawn a lion two nights back? Yesterday he drew the same lion to me and said that the it had moved from where it was. He says he has been noticing other pictures of his move too and the two of us were wondering what could be the reason for that."

"And what did you conclude?" asked Sita with great excitement and interest.

"He says that the stars in the sky must by similar to the sun and the moon in the sky, but much smaller. That's why they move slower than the sun or the moon. They might be like ants in the sky and the moon might be the elephant."

"So there is another world just like ours up there?"

"Nobody knows."

The two of them reached the shore after half an hour and Laxman walked back home. Sita however had an important task to complete before she headed home.

She adorned another dress that she had brought with her and stood facing the reflection of the moon in the river. She closed her eyes and when the beating of her heart became the only sound she could hear – Sita began to sing. And that announced the arrival of a new day for the forest around her.

Her voice, sweeter than the Mambazham, more melodious than the chirping sparrow, a beauty that may embarrass the dazzling moonlight that dances in the river; it poured out of her voice, one single note. And from there she escalated to another note, one by one, up and down and the forest received a rainfall of music. Crisp notes that echoed from the trees and reflected the stillness that blanketed her, very slow, very gentle, which she peppered with subtle nuances that sometimes made everyone look up and some other times, merged with the rhythm of her voice and sank in the ocean of music that Sita created.

She had lost herself into the magic for a full hour and when she finally opened her eyes, she saw a dozen of her dear friends sitting around her, just physically, waking up only when she finished her recital.

"That was TOOO Good Sita. When do you start singing? Today I ran towards to river as early as possible and still missed the beginning of your melody."

"How do you do it Sita? How do you manage to hypnotise every soul around you? What is the magic in your voice? Teach us too know." 12 beautiful girls, brown skinned like the bark of teak and possessing a glow even in the middle of the night; sat around her, as close to her as possible.

"Hey, why didn't you dance today?" One of the girls asked with a smile.

"Umm..." Sita answered, "I didn't feel like. I don't know, the dance and the music... It has to come from inside me. I can't dance at will."

"You can try. Seeing your dance after the song will make us feel complete. Like having a full meal prepared by Drupa."

"Ohh, no! My art cannot compare to the food of my father!"

"You are being modest. Or maybe it is because you haven't seen yourself dance. It is just.... Too much!"

"But... Not today guys..." The stillness she had witnessed in the morning was consuming Sita. She had fully absorbed the beauty of that silence and reproduced it through her song.

"Please Sita... For your fans!"

"Fans? I am no Dev"

"You are so much prettier. And make us much more happier!"

"Come on Sita. I will dance with you", it was Malati who spoke, pulling her hand up.

"I will sing for you. Nothing like what you do, but just for support", Devi sat up. "What do you want me to sing?"

Sita stood up but couldn't move. She looked around her for help... and she got the help. A quick breeze brushed her face and let her long hair fly. She looked across the river and saw the trees sway in the wind, their leaves shivering above them. Her body imitated the scenery. For the delight of her fans, Sita danced in tune to the wind, slowly swaying her hips, raising both her hands above head and vibrating her fingers like the hundreds of leaves above her. Devi too felt the breeze on her face and began her song. Malati followed her friends lead. The other girls stood up and danced along.

A group danced ensued and the rest of the girls repeated their favourite opening step and Sita along with Malati continued to move at the command of the wind and under Devi's guidance. They moved forward to step into the water and splashed it around with their feet – millions of water droplets sprayed around, each droplet reflecting the moonlight and the dancing girls became the backdrop for the scene. As Sita went round and round, her dress being raised a little by the wind, her feet on the ground as light as a feather, she leaped towards the moon and the others did too.

"Oops... guess we are late!" Sita realised quickly and turned around. The other girls who were still dancing merrily, suddenly stopped and dived into the water. Sita stepped up towards the bank where she stopped for a second to look at herself in the mirror. "You look beautiful", her friends kept saying again and again in her head and she wanted to see it for herself.

The river showed her a dark face, brown, but darker than her peers. Her eyes were huge and resembled a swan. She was just as tall as the other girls in her village were, and had a perfect curvy figure, something she earned from the many hours of dance she did. And beside her waist, she could see the tip of her lush long hair which was being blown to one side by the wind. In between her thick hair, invisible to anybody's eyes, rested a single white feather of an unknown bird.

Sita entered her house just as her father lit the firewood and breakfast was getting ready. Her mother, who happened to be the head of the village, was off to the marketplace to supervise trade. Her job as the village leader included determining the prices of various items being traded in the market and to ensure that the barter was righteous. How much cloth was to be exchanged for a certain amount of rice? How much cloth would have to be exchanged for the same amount of wheat? Most often the people came to a consensus by themselves, but in case of a dispute, maybe because one of the traders had an urgent requirement, or maybe a new product was being sold in the market, Arundhathi would be the one to take a decision. And nobody opposed her decisions, not just because she was the village leader, but because her decisions always proved to be right. Arundhathi had a deep knowledge of all kinds of trade and personally knew each and every villagers, their strengths and weaknesses, their sufferings and pain and had an uncanny skill of serving justice.

Further, she was to be addressed for any difficult that arose in the village. If a cow died, or some crops failed, or when everything was lost in the flood, if a house was destroyed – Arundhathi would be the one to meet. And she never failed her people. Whoever was in trouble, whoever needed a helping hand, she managed to give it. If not from her own resources, she arranged help from the resources of fellow villagers.

And when a fellow villager was asked for help, she was more than ready to offer; even more than she could afford to. It was a generous village (a prosperous one too)and everybody loved their neighbour like their family. And family loved each other from the depths if its soul.

After trade was over in the morning Arundhathi returned home to help her husband who had finished cooking breakfast. Sita and Laxman sat in the kitchen, greedily tasting their father's masterpiece. "What are you two doing?" The mother enquired.

"I just asked them to see if it tastes good", Drupa answered.

Arundhathi responded with a laugh, "When has your preparation been anything less than perfect? Don't let the kids steal all the food." She turned to her children and said sarcastically, "Now if you feel everything is alright, can we serve breakfast?"

Outside their house, over a hundred people gathered and sat on the ground in 5 rows. Laxman grabbed the clay plates from his workplace which was just a few metres from the house and began placing a plate in front of each person. After the plates were distributed, Drupa, his wife and two children, along with the help of a few other villagers who volunteered to help, served breakfast to the crowd.

Most villagers had a kitchen in their house and also had the means to cook their own meal too, but at least once a day, they wanted to be fed by Drupa. This was a tradition that the village followed since Drupa was 20. The fame of his food had gone across all the five villages and spread throughout the civilisation, that almost once in every five days, people would flock from the neighbouring villages to feast themselves.

It was one such feast, before Drupa had taken it up as a profession, that he met Arundhathi and fell for her, head over heels. Or rather, she fell for him. After that day, Arundhathi insisted that she be fed by Drupa every day. And she also demanded that her friends too have a taste of the maestro's art.

"Hey Arundhathi", one day, Drupa finally told the woman of his dreams, "I am really flattered that you feel I am such a good cook. And I really enjoying feeding all your friends. But I am really sorry; I cannot afford to do so anymore. My family cannot afford this much."

"But Drupa..." Arundhathi pleaded, "your food must be the finest in the world. It would be a crime if you can't feed everybody. Everybody deserves to be fed by you. How selfish would it be if your talents could serve only your family?"

"I know. And I guess I can throw a party once in a while. But this can't go on every day. Tell me yourself, how can I arrange for all the supplies?"

"Well", and thus, Arundhathi the master of trade was born. "You just worry about the cooking. I will arrange for the supplies."

"You -"

"Trust me... I will manage everything." Arundhathi felt the villagers were being denied justice, and she decided to serve it in the form of three meals a day. She told all the village folk that they would be served three mouth watering meals a day and all they had to do was contribute something in return. "Have the food and contribute what you think he deserves", she announced. "She didn't announce anything. She cast a spell on the village." Drupa recollected his story and told his children.

"Your father is a great cook because he feeds the heart. Into every piece of vegetable that he adds in the dish, he pours his heart, he pours his love and care.

He just doesn't feed people, but he actually cares for them. And the villagers might call me the leader, but I always feel Drupa will make a much better leader. He is full of love. Nobody can care for the village like he can."

The success story of Drupa and Arundhathi inspired every child to go beyond the walls of their home and give something to the village. And as Sita chose dance and music as her profession, and Laxman chose sculpture as his profession, children extrapolated their imagination to new heights and began to brew wonders in the village.

Das, the astronomer is one such example. Anurag, another friend of Sita and Laxman transforms tools into machines. Anurag's mechanical skills and Laxman's acumen in sculptures enabled them to improve the tools that villagers used on a daily basis. Bullock carts moved faster and ploughs that dug deeper became lighter. Anurag made it easier to extract water from the well and also helped build the first common bath in the village.

That evening the market was cleared, a fire was made in the middle and Sita performed to her delight. The villagers watched in awe as the beautiful girl gyrated before the fire, the fiery heat inspired and energized her, and the dance brought a spark to every man's heart. And the dance went on, deep into the night.

In a far off desert, an army lead by a young prince moved in search of its next conquest. A hundred horses and a hundred camels, followed by a hundred soldiers on foot moved under merciless heat. They were followed by twenty palanquins carrying women of royal blood. However, what slowed the journey was the dazzling amount of gold that traversed the desert with them.

The army was majestic and formidable, but the forces of nature weakened them. The gold which they adorned as a show of their glory began to weigh upon them. As the food and water began to trickle, the prince who lead them faced a nightmare.

"We won't survive for more than a week", one of the ministers informed.

"The king is asking if we are lost", another minister asked.

"Yes. Yes, we are, but nobody else needs to know that", the prince commanded.

Greed had lead them into the desert in search of a paradise that flooded with gold. Little did they know the treasure that awaited them was nothing but vengeance. Vengeance for the plunders they had committed.

For Laxman it all started with clay, a solid form that stood somewhere between being mud or a stone. It was mud that could be harndened to become stone – in whatever shape you like. And Laxman loved shapes. He was a child prodigy at clay modelling and as he grew old enough to handle a chisel, even wood and stone transformed into life like things. His workplace, a rectangular room built by him with the help of Anurag was decorated by statues made by him on every corner. The roofs were thatched with quite a few opening that always kept the room bright and the door was built with bamboo. One of the walls consisted of several tiny statues stacked one above the other and the opposite wall consisted of crockery, tools and other stuff which he used himself or sold to others. The wall opposite the door had the largest statues made by him, in the middle of them all, like a queen, stood the dancing statue of his sister – her hair flying to one side and her clothes fluttering in the wind. It was bigger than life size, built on grey stone, and was undoubtedly the centre of attraction at the workplace.

Sitting in the middle of his room with his tools, stone and clay, all neatly arranged around him just like his father handled food, Laxman was busy at work after lunch chiselling a piece of rock, when he heard the hooves of a horse run past his room towards his home. Laxman stood up a and followed the voice.

A messenger had come from the neighbouring town with a message for his mother. "I believe you have recognised me."

"Oh yes I do", Arundhathi, who never forgot a face, asked, "How is everyone at home? And I assume you are on an official visit. What is the matter?" Lunch was just over and Arundhathi was cleaning the house before attending to her cattle for mid-day milking.

"For the past three weeks we have been observing a tribe move through the desert across the forest on our northern side. At first we thought they were approaching our village but then we noticed that they were just passing by. We thought of ignoring them at first but then Thapa", Thapa was the leader of the northern most village in the civilisation, from where the messenger had come, "felt something wrong. He asked some of the travellers from our village and neighbouring village if there were any other villages in the neighbourhood and he was informed that there were none. This worried Thapa.

"He immediately sent my brother on a horse to ensure that the tribe that was passing by had enough supplies and to invite them to our village if they wanted to rest or have a refill of supplies. Oh! It seems I have just missed lunch", the messenger, asked Arundhathi noticing her husband carry the washed plates towards his son's room.

"Yes, we just finished. I almost forgot to ask, have you had your lunch?" Arundhathi quickly recollected if they had any left-over and if not, whether Drupa can quickly arrange a snack for the visitor.

"That is really nice of you, but I had lunch on the way. Although I do regret missing Drupa's meal. Guess I should I have started a little earlier."

"No villager should miss Drupa's meal. Not if he has wished for it."

"That is all I know to do, and all I like to do. Please take your seat, I will arrange a quick bite for you." Drupa, who returned from his son's masonry, joined his wife and said.

"Oh please Drupa. I don't think that will be necessary. I did have a heartening meal on the way and I don't think there is room for any more."

"We insist." Arundhathi said.

"And you know very well that nobody can refuse that", the messenger said with a laugh and took his seat outside the house. Drupa turned around and entered his kitchen, while Arundhathi and Laxman readied a seat and brought a plate.

After the snack that Drupa arranged in no time and the messenger, whom Arundhathi recalled was named Arav, hungrily finished it off, they exchanged compliments and Arav continued.

"My brother took three days to reach them, only to find that they had stopped moving as the entire tribe was completely drained off of food, water and energy, and any strength left in them was sucked up by the scorching sun and the blazing sand. Without another thought, my brother, Irav, invited all of them over to our village." Arundhathi and Laxman nodded in agreement to what Arav was saying.

"They just reached our village yesterday evening and we fed them and made arrangements for them to stay for the night. Today morning – one of the older men in the tribe, probably their leader talked to Thapa and Thapa informed them about our civilisation, about our five villages. And then..." Arav paused for a second and continued, "The old man asked Thapa that he wanted to meet the leader of our civilisation. Thapa told him that there was no such single leader.

"And then he asked us which was the biggest and richest village. Thapa felt that they wanted to stay with us for a while and assumed that they felt our village was not capable of accommodating them and hence he raised this question. He thought carefully and told them about your village. But before he sends them over here, he wanted to know if you were indeed ready to take them in."

"What kind of question is that? Of course we are ready to give them shelter. They can stay here as long as they like. And if there are too many of them then we can arrange for more food and necessaries. That is no problem at all."

"There are around a hundred horses, a hundred camels and around three hundred people. And they seem to carry a lot of supplies with them too, but when asked about it, they didn't say anything. Apparently it is something they protect very dearly. We don't know anything else."

"When will they arrive?" Arundhathi asked.

"I will reach there today evening and let them know your consent. Thapa won't let them travel at night, so I guess they will start tomorrow morning after breakfast and arrive here for lunch."

"Drupa will be waiting", Arundhathi said with a sly smile at her husband. Drupa on the other was visibly excited at the idea of feeding another 300 people. But the horses worried him.

"What will we do about the animals?" Drupa enquired.

"I will talk to the people at the market about this and see who can contribute what. If we are short of supplies, we can send a few people to collect food from the forest, there is nothing to worry about." Arundhathi rhymed and began calculating the amount of extra supplies she would have to arrange from the next day onwards; and the source of those supplies.

The next day a huge procession entered the village and met Arundhathi at the open field where the forest ended. A crowd, just as big as the incoming tribe was waiting to welcome their guest. Most of them were however curious about the tribe that rode with a hundred horses and a hundred camels carrying mysterious goods (the village was small and held no secrets.)

And the curiosity was justified, or maybe, multiplied manifold as a young man with wheat coloured skin, light brown eyes, thick long hair reaching his shoulders, clean shaven face (in contrast to all the village men who were bearded) and adorned with heavy clothes that sparkled in the sun. He rode a horse which was also dressed up in gold like the young man. He was followed by few other men, who looked darker and wore lesser clothes than him, following him on foot and then slowly, the entire tribe emerged from the forest. Very few men looked like the prince and rode on horses, and none of them sparkled as much as he did. Most of the men were on foot and darker than the horse riders, but still their skin was much lighter than the villagers.

The men on foot were accompanied by well dressed horses and camels that carried huge shining boxes which clearly proved that the animals were very strong. And behind them the men on foot carried heavy boxes, four men holding the extended corners of the box, and walked steadily with the load. All the huge boxes were placed in the middle of the procession, with men carrying sharp edged sticks standing close to it wearing a grim expression on their face. Only one such box was brought forward and placed on the ground in front of the young man. And from within the box an old man emerged, dressed even more glamorously than the young man behind him (many of the village youngsters got engaged in a debate, whether the attire was glamorous or comical) with a heavy hat placed on his head and a thick white moustache, as white as a pigeon, and a huge belly that scared many kids.

But the mysteries and wonders of the sights she beheld did not startle Arundhathi. With a pleasant smile, like a respectable host, she welcomed the funny looking man. "How was the journey for you and your people?"

The old man seemed to be shocked at the question and answered in a slow, thick voice. "A rather long one. Can I meet your leader?"

"Well, the people around here call me the village leader. I can speak on behalf of the village. And may I know whom I am speaking to?"

The king couldn't believe that the village had a woman as the leader. In his nation, it was almost blasphemous for a woman to show her face to the sun, and the old man was never lenient to such crimes. He turned around to look at his son, who was observing the scene intensely.

"I am King Rajagupta Arya of the Aryan clan", the King announced gloriously. "We come from across the desert in search of a new home."

Arundhathi spoke with a smile that continued to glow, "If you believe that our village can suit your convenience, then please make yourself at home." Arundhathi was indeed worried about the repercussions of accommodating so many more people in their village. So many more houses would have to built, forest would have to be cleared for agriculture, the marketplace would have to be expanded, and continuous supplies must be ensured. But those issues were a second priority, and saying no to those who came with a request was impossible for her. Not just Arundhathi who had a flair for justice, but every villager who was taught to love and care for others would do what she did. Welcome them home right away!

And her welcome shocked the king again. Two parallel thoughts ran in his mind: "I was expecting a war over here. I had asked my son to be prepared for that. But these people, instead of asking me to get out, they are welcoming me?"

On the other side of his mind: "This is why women are not allowed to step out of their homes. They cannot even protect themselves, how can one expect them to protect a nation. This village has really stupid people indeed."

"But I guess we can have a detailed conversation later. You have had a long and tiring journey, why don't we serve lunch for you."

Drupa's house was clearly not sufficient to host the entire tribe so the market place was cleared and necessary arrangements were made to serve lunch. None of the other villagers feasted Drupa's meal that day and many of them volunteered to help make the new comers feel at home. News had spread already that the visitors had intentions of making the village their new home, and all of them were excited at the prospect of having new neighbours, that too, people with such bright skin. "So cruel of me. How could I even think of supplies and other obstacles when everybody else is so excited?" Arundhathi thought for a second. The truth however was that nobody was ever concerned about a shortfall of supplies. They always had a magnificent leader who made sure that food, clothing, shelter and anything else they would ever need was aplenty.

As the villagers built naive dreams about a bigger village with more friends and relatives and as the king schemed for diabolic conquest of the rich and plentiful paradise he had set eyes on, only the prince observed the scene with wisdom and acumen.

Adithya, the young prince, had interpreted the very first sign of welcome itself with fear and doubt. They had been sent to the desert by one of the wise men of their empire in search of a – "Paradise beyond your wildest dreams, where brass turns into gold and stones turn into diamond. Where monuments and forts reach the sky and where clothes are softer than feather." As the empire was at the verge of a civil war with the people revolting against the rulers and the army divided into factions, the king and the prince decided to flee the nation carrying all the gold the treasury possessed with all the slaves, the palace women and all the horses and camels that they would require in the journey.

But after the second day itself, the prince realised the trap they had fallen into and dreaded a merciless death. However, he kept his fears to himself and continued to lead the army in search of a dream world.

At last, when all the food was over, when all the water had dried up and the king himself had to starve, a messenger arrived on a horse and invited them, offering food and shelter. The very first thought in the prince' mind, "They don't want to just starve us to death. It is going to be a painful death. This is a most certain ambush", and he almost killed the messenger. But then what? Death was imminent and if there is a fraction of truth in the messenger's words, it would be worth the risk. He immediately asked the army commander, "Get ready for an ambush. Don't mind the heat, put on your armour and have your swords at the ready. And ask the soldiers, if worse comes to worst, kill the women and kill themselves. We may lose lives but we can't lose honour."

Cautiously the prince moved with his army and his ignorant father and entered a village... A village where even the wind cooed – "Paradise!" For a moment, the prince was blinded.

As the army moved south, the desert sand began to thicken into mud and slowly turned green, grass growing around them with every step they took and the sun cooling down as the trees blessed them with shade. The greenery grew into a forest, so thick that the entire army had to move in single file until they reached the banks of a magnificent river. And across the river, the sight was heavenly. Vast fields of paddy, rice, wheat and grass, one after the other, interspersed with tall trees and brilliant flowers that won the awes of all, everything in the backdrop of a lush green mountain range that touched the clouds and poured water into the ground.

They were fed by Irav at the bank with some fruits he managed to collect with the help of the soldiers from the surrounding trees, a delightful snack even for those of royal standards. One by one, the Aryan clan crossed the river in rafts and reach the other side, where not just the eyes, but every sense organ was feasted with delight. With thick forest on all three sides and magnificent agriculture at the end, the cool river which flowed with glistening blue water, the flowers all around them that flushed the atmosphere with an aroma which might even draw honey bees from their own empire, some birds chirping invisibly and the others displaying the glory in the sky as they glided across the sun putting a well choreographed display of shapes, the swans settling around the rafts to greet the new comers, the sweetness of the fruits they ate, fish dancing under their feet and the never-ending greenness that they approached – for a moment Adithya relaxed, "Maybe we were not lied to. Maybe..." Just for a moment.

But nature it seems, was determined to prove the prince wrong as the villagers welcomed the clan with wide open arms and Thapa insisting that they be as comfortable as royalty. His father mistook the courtesy for slavery and demanded to meet the king of the village and ask them to surrender before his army. But Adithya was not so naive. If the people are so rich, they would have thought of something to protect it. He looked around constantly in search of swords of spears, but none caught his eyes. At night he barely slept and did not remove his armour either.

After a day, they travelled to what, as they were informed, was their capital city. King Rajagupta wanted to talk to their King what they would want in return for surrendering their kingdom to the Aryan clan. There again, both father and son were surprised. Both of them expected the king to pull out his sword and announce a battle cry when Rajagupta said, "We are looking for a new home", but instead their queen, asked them to see if the kingdom was worth their presence and fed them.

Throughout lunch, Adithya was mesmerised at the sights around him. The city was rich, nobody was starving, nobody was poor, nobody was homeless, nobody was sick and yet, there were plenty of trees all around. He was astounded at the way civilisation and nature were married in the village, as people took immaculate care of preserving the forest green as it was and also managing to build as many houses as they required, create as many paddy fields as they wanted and feed as many cattle as they needed.

The people too were nothing like he had expected. As a matter of fact, they were beyond his wildest dreams. The woman who had introduced herself as the queen was helping the peasants in serving lunch and cleaning up after them.

"How much do you think we should offer them to buy all this land. It doesn't look like they have any defence, we can simply ask them to run away and find some other place to live. And if they want to live here, they can live as our slaves. The army is ready is it not."

"No", Adithya said quickly. "I mean... not yet." He thought for a moment and said, "Didn't you notice their leader, the queen. How she said that we can live here only if we feel the village will suit our convenience. We have to first make sure that this is the right place for us. Let me look around, study the empire, see if they have any gold or not, and then we will think of a conquest. Till then, you can inform them that we would stay here as guest."

"Why go through all the trouble? You have a sword in your arsenal. Slash them off and run along. You have nothing to lose."

"Father please, believe me. This place looks too good to be... defenceless! I am sure they have an army and I want to be well prepared if we are planning an attack.

"Look at the queen. Does she look like one? She is bowing before our soldiers to serve them."    "She    is just an imposter. There is something fishy around here. Something doesn't add up, something doesn't seem to be right. Father, for now I want you to just protect yourself and stay safe. We will strike when the time comes."

# Chapter 5

# Conflict

Sita made her way through the newly built temporary huts along the paddy fields towards the semi-brick house that was constructed in one night to accommodate the Aryan prince. She too had worked all night to arrange accommodation for all the soldiers and the royal guest, not to mention the food and clothing for them and the animals too.

After lunch the previous day, the king had expressed his interest in knowing the way of life of the civilisation they were visiting and Arundhathi promptly delegated the task to her daughter, who, since the arrival of the Aryan army was the front runner in making arrangements for their stay and coaching fellow villagers in hospitality management.

"We will let them have their meals before us", "We will need more people to volunteer in serving food", "Get the market place cleared quickly", "We will have to split our jobs. You people go and help father with dinner, while we go and build some shade for them to sleep at night", "Don't use up all the wood for their houses. Use some to build a fencing for their cattle." Displaying features that made many villagers say in their hearts, "I think we have successor for Arundhathi already", Sita lead the village through an ordeal that could have easily turned into a crisis. Of course, nobody had a clue of how tragic a crisis things could possibly turn into.

On the other end of the vast fields of the village, Adithya was given a house to stay, one of the only few that was built in brick the previous night. After her bath, cutting short her morning concert, she reached the prince' chambers well before sunrise to find him in deep slumber. May not be up to royal standards, but the villagers had managed to give him a comfortable sleep.

Slowly she entered the room, carefully placing her foot on the ground and making sure she made no sound, she reached the prince' bed and wondered, "How do I wake him up now?" She bent down to her knees and stretched her arm forward to touch his cheek. And as her fingers made contact with the glowing skin of his face, the prince drew his sword from under the bed in a flash and pushed it towards her neck, not chopping her head off only by a matter of milliseconds. The sword was held firmly pressed against her neck.

But Sita didn't flinch. Even as Adithya's eyes drilled into hers and the deadly weapon still placed on her neck, Sita only looked back at him with curious intensity and just before the situation turned awkward, she smiled at him and said, "Good morning. Don't you want to have your bath?"

Her sweet voice poured like honey into his ears for sure, but it was the courage with which she smiled back at him even with the sword on her neck that really shook him. It wasn't just a courteous gesture, it was a smile that came from the heart and demanded one in return. Adithya however, didn't oblige. On a serious note he asked with his thick voice, "It is still dark"

"We start the day at this time. Breakfast will be served at dawn, so you have to be clean and ready in front of our house by then. Come on, I will take you to the river. There is a spot across the fields, a little away from the market through the forest which might impress you. Not many people go there to swim but it is a beautiful place. You will see", Sita said and withdrew from the hut. "Hurry up", she added before she walked through the curtains that made a door for the princely chambers.

A woman who spoke with so much confidence and yet sounded so polite. Adithya, convinced that the village had many more surprises to offer, overcome by curiosity, quickly got up and followed the princess outside.

Sita walked with him through the vast forests which showed greenery as long as the eyes could see on both sides. "Harvest season is yet to come. Another three months I guess. Most of the villagers are engaged in agriculture. And that indeed drives our society." Sita began to talk about the different crops season, the agriculture process, the various crops that were grown and boasted about the tools that her brother had built with Anurag, to which Adithya listened with intense astonishment.

But he realised that the mysteries of Sita's world were only beginning to reveal themselves as the two entered the forest and he looked around him at the millions of plants and animals that let them pass through the narrow path in the forest. Monkeys and birds looked at them from above in the dark and warmly welcomed the visitors. Even though the sun had not lit the day, the colourful flowers that bloomed in the forest were visible. The huge trees with invisible tops roofed them. "Malati, I guess, would have been a better tour guide for you. She knows the name of each and every leaf that grows over here and also its uses, dangers, benefits and anything else you would want to know. Do you have these plants in your home?"

Home? The word made Adithya uneasy. Even as the rulers of the desert oasis where he and his father were born and raised, neither of them had felt a homely attachment to the place. The love the villagers tended to their land, the care with they did agriculture and now as Sita explained to them about her friends who knew the forest so well, "like the back of her hand", as Sita put it. All of that were new lessons that Adithya learnt hungrily.

"No, our kingdom was not so green." Sita laughed at his response and the laugh turned into a hum which grew into a song which made the parrots, pigeons, sparrows, love birds, owls, doves, monkeys, squirrels, rabbits, chameleons, foxes, cats and dogs to hover around them. One of the sparrows joined the song with its own chirp and settled on her hand, and the other birds gave a chorus with the flutter of their wings. Sita dropped a few *Coos* in her song and the pigeons responded with their own *Coos.*

"Are you talking to them?" Adithya asked Sita in the middle of the song. "Oh yeah!" Sita sang and moved her song to the next octave.

The entire forest had come to life, the leaves rustled all around and branches cracked above them, which almost made the prince pull out in sword. Many of the fairy tale animals made their presence in front of the human duo, and each animal that ran around them, sometimes through the middle of their feet, made Adithya flinch with a tinge of fear. But that vanished soon, as he too couldn't help but tap his feet.

The song ended at Sita's highest note as the two of them emerged from the forest to the calm bank of their mother river. "She gives us water, she gives us life. We give her nothing more than respect. Just like a mother! You know to swim don't you?"

"No, not yet", said Adithya and tried to dive into the water which ended up as a clumsy jump. The water was flowing and Adithya struggled to find air, but before Sita pushed the panic button and dived in to save him, Adithya seemed to have got the hang of it. Keeping his nose above the water, that is. And slowly he moved his arms and legs to find his way through the water. Sita smiled in relief. And then laughed at the clothes Adithya had worn for his swim – his very own battle armour.

"Why don't you remove it? I will get you some new clothes."

"That won't be required"

"So what do you intend to wear after your bath."

At his palace, his servants would decide that for him. "I am not removing my armour. Not yet." Adithya said. Sita didn't ask further questions. He swam a short distance and then reached back to his tour guide who walked him back in his wet clothes. "The sun is almost up. It's breakfast time." Sita regretted missing the opportunity of being with his father as he waved his wand over the cooking dish.

After breakfast Adithya dropped in to visit his sister in her palanquin, who sat along with the other women, denied access to show their face outside the curtains of the vehicle. As Adithi, the young princess grumbled and complained about not being able to even have a proper bath, Adithya added to the fears of the other woman and increased her complains by talking about the dangers of the forest around her and the mysterious army that could attack them any moment.

Depressed with complaints, Adithya went ahead to meet his army which was accommodated in small huts and the soldiers had to adjust in an extremely congested living space, which was certainly better than the battle zone and the blazing desert they were used to, but they too complained about the situation they were put in and the difficulties they were going through. Adithya couldn't help feeling guilty because the villagers had built just the right number of huts, but the king and his ministers took up all the large huts leaving the soldiers with limited means. And the guilt stung him like never before because of what he had seen at breakfast.

Nobody was separate, nobody was different and nobody demanded superiority in the village. There was equality as he had never witnessed before, and even when they built the huts for their guest, they expected the same level of equality from the Aryan clan.

"But we are royalty and deserve better, don't we?" Such questions and many more including, "How can a woman lead so many people?", "Is it right for women to walk about freely? That too in the forest?", "How does their pride allow them to do such lowly jobs like cleaning dishes and washing clothes?" and some more perverted ones like, "Was the girl trying to woo me today morning? Was she inviting me when she walked into my room and later when she asked me to remove my clothes at the river?".

"Adithya?" Laxman caught up to the prince walking outside the soldiers' quarters. As Adithya looked up Laxman smiled and said, "Come on. You said you wanted to learn the village right? The guy you have to meet is Anurag. He will stun you!" Laxman said modestly and lead him to his friend.

The entire day, Adithya spent marvelling at the miracles built by the young men. He looked at every tool built by Anurag and Laxman and analysed them carefully, like a little child looking at his new toy, one that nobody else had in the neighbourhood. His brain rushed through the details of the machines that he was shown, understood the simplicity and elegance of the design and wondered about how much better it made life for them or in another sense, how much worse his own life was? Even more deeply, he wondered about the kind of creative and muscular effort that they might have put to make the tools. Why hadn't anyone in his nation thought of it. "They did build some new weapons", Adithya tried to tell himself positively but his heart wasn't convinced.

As he saw the sun set, Adithya told his friends 'Good Night', promising them that he would be back the next day to see the machines, and walked out of Anurag's workshop towards his sister's palanquin. He was half hearted about his visit as he knew that the excitement of learning a new science would be shattered in moments by his sisters frustration and depression. Adithya however was shocked to see a beautiful girl with a glowing smile behind the curtain of Adithi's chambers.

"Oh! You are back? How was your day?" Adithi enquired his brother in cheerful tone, a tone that he never knew existed.

"It was great actually. How was yours?" Adithya was curious about the mood her sister was in, but that didn't last long as he sister set off on a marathon speech about how she spent her time with her new friend – "Her name is Sita. The really dark girl with long hair. She told me she met you today morning."

So her name is Sita, Adithya thought to himself and thanked her for the invaluable service she had done to him. More deeply, he thanked her for bringing a joy to Adithi that he had never seen. "When I told her I wanted to walk in the forest she asked me to come with her. But then I said I couldn't so she rushed outside and in five minutes brought me some fifty different flowers of different colours and shapes and sizes. And along with her came two three cute little animals which nibbled me so tenderly and when I took them on my hands, it was so nice, their furry skin and little claws on my palm. And they looked so amazing, I asked her if I could keep it with me... then she said it can stay here as long as it wants. But when Sita left, the little animal... the squirrel went along with it. I almost cried as it left me, so Sita promised that she would bring back the squirrel tomorrow for me to play with. And she gave all of us, all the girls these bright flowers. Ahh... they smell so beautiful!"

The atmosphere was almost similar at the soldiers room and Adithya felt the dark princess' footprints over there too. "You guys seem to be in a better mood?

Jayant offered a salary boost?" Raghav was their army commander.

"No nothing of the sort," one of the senior men in the army replied. "We all just started liking the place. A girl came here and showed us around. The river and the forest and all that. Not such a bad place after all."

Another soldier asked with a puppy-dog face that didn't exactly suit a soldier, but the expression was just that. "Will we be here for while?"

"I don't know. Whom did you say showed you around?"

"That really dark girl with long hair", the older man said.

"And really beautiful hips", another soldier added.

For a moment Adithya thanked her again, but then his heart got carried away by the questions that popped in his mind. "What kind of woman is she? How could she shamelessly expose herself before so many men? How could she bring herself to give company to these kind of men?" Adithya thought with disgust and also agreed that her dark skin made her more beautiful. His honour stopped his mind from going any further.

That night Adithya made his way home under the half moon that was accompanied by a few neatly shaped clouds and thousands of twinkling stars which seemed to talk to him. Little did he know that in the other side of the village, it actually did talk to someone. Das was so close to revealing the mystery behind the shape of the moon and the movement of the stars.

"So, how was the day?" Sita called out to him from behind. Adithya looked at her with contempt and continued walking. "What was that on your face?

Disgust or sorrow. Laxman was telling me that you had a good time."

"What do you want with me?" Adithya spit it out bluntly.

"I just want to know if my guest is having a god time", Sita stepped in front of him and asked.

"That is very polite of you – Sita. Thank you. I did have a fine day", Adithya said in an evidently formal tone.

"Glad, I also wanted to ask what you wanted to do tomorrow. Stay at the workshop with Anurag, or see the market with my mother?"

Adithya had made it certain that he would spend another day with Anurag but the second option seemed too irresistible. How all of them filled their tummy – that was a question that haunted him since the minute he stepped into the village. "The market", he answered.

"I will let her know", Sita said and almost started when she added, "and just because a girl talks to men, or even spends time with them, it doesn't make her a bad girl."

Adithya looked at her with a dropped jaw. Sita continued, "And in our village we all hope, that men have the strength to treat women with respect. I pray that every human has the strength to restrain himself. The men of our village do. Good Night."

Sita's remarks were however directed less to herself and more towards the way the Aryans had locked up all their women. But she could also read Adithya's mind and the prejudice he held towards women in general and to herself, specifically.

Laxman had often told her about how his friends were carried away whenever she danced. Her performance were never sensuous but her brother frankly admitted that some men of a certain age couldn't help but be arisen by her presence. Sita's family believed in the guidance and support that an invisible and incomprehensible force gave the village, but Sita herself had little interest in something she didn't feel was important. However, since her brother's remarks, she prayed to god every time she danced that God give the men the strength of restrain. That was the only thing she ever asked for. "It is the only thing worth praying", she often said. It was that very prayer that gave her courage as Adithya's sword was slashed at her and pressed against her neck.

Through her conversation with the Aryan princess and from the glance of disgust that Adithya had on her face as he heard her voice, Sita deduced that he was pathetically prejudiced towards women and felt she should share a piece of her mind with him. It did do him a lot of good as he entered the house telling himself, "She is a really wise girl. A really brave girl." The image of Sita smiling at him with his sword on her neck appeared before him.

Within the few hours he spent in the forest village, Adithya understood that their way of life was as different from his own as a potato and a goldfish, thus, the new morning began with a resolve to forget everything he knew till then and learn all over again. Adithya shed all the ego the prince possessed and transformed into a child ready to drink in everything around him. Why such a resolution? Probably his heart told him... that it is worth a shot.

He saw Sita in the morning, serving his soldiers at breakfast and smiled at her, which she returned politely. After breakfast, followed Arundhathi to the market where she told him about her work and how one was to go about it. "You need to know who has how much and who needs how much. My job is not so difficult, because every villager is a friend and we all live as a family over here. I know by-heart who can sell what and who can buy what, and simply catalyse the process by directly the sellers to the buyers. And if somebody has an urgent requirement, I arrange for a loan and if somebody is not satisfied with the price he gets, I do something to help him or her out. And then there are those people who don't exactly make anything or sell things, like my husband or myself. We live on the contribution made by the villagers for our services. They give what they think we are worth. And most often it is way more than we require or, to be honest, what I think we are worth."

Adithya suddenly thought of Sita and her music in the forest. "So everybody does something?"

"Yes, something that the village needs. Or the village wants. Or sometimes, they do things simply for their own amusement, simply because they like doing it. For example there is a boy named Das in the village. All he does is gaze at the sky, all the time. He sleeps during the day and is awake, gazing at the stars all night. The youngsters in the village really admire him because he draws pictures or something in the sky."

"Pictures in the sky?"

"I know, it is crazy. We adults of the village had a debate about what should be done with him. We had no idea how gazing at the sky would serve the village. However, it was finally decided that everybody has the right to do what they like. We decided to provide for him out of the common supplies at the village."

"So is he not a liability for you."

"Anurag and Laxman are the ones to look up to. Even when they started building things, Anurag mechanically and Laxman artistically, we had no clue how it would serve anything. But in time they proved to build miracles. Anurag made life so much easier for us, and Laxman made us so proud of ourselves. His statues and idols that depict the village life and the way he works actually makes the village move. We hope that one day Das too will give us a miracle." Adithya contemplated in silence when Arundhathi added, "Is that not two things that keeps everyone afloat. A hope for the best. And the opportunity to do what you love? Isn't that life?"

The question was not rhetorical for Adithya. Her words had pushed him into a tide of thoughts which flowed from the things he liked, to the things he did and the hopes he had. And he drew a sharp contrast with the life of any of the villagers – Sita for instance.

"What does Sita do?"

"She does what others like", Arundhathi said and laughed. "There is nothing she likes. She will do anything to make others happy, that is her special skill. People say she is gifted with music and dance, but what I feel proud of is her ability to cheer people up. That is what, if you ask me, makes her sing or dance."

Sita's voice echoed in his ears again and again, the rustling of the leaves, cooing birds, buzzing insects; the entire forest was brought to life and danced before her. "A person who makes others happy", Adithya thought of his plunders and loots, the riots of his people, the wars he had waged and the blood he had shed. He thought of the tears he would have brought, of which he had no idea, of which he never thought. "She brings smiles and I bring tears."

After lunch Adithya walked to his sister's palanquin and saw her in high spirits. As expected, Sita was inside. At his entrance, both of them became silent. Adithya looked at the two and asked, "Where are the other women?"

"They are having a nap after lunch. I too was supposed to but then Sita dropped by so we were just having fun."

A request that was brimming on Sita's lips came out of Adithya's in the form of an answer, "Why don't you show my sister around then?"

A glow appeared on both their faces. They turned to each other showing all 32 teeth in a brilliant smile and Adithi turned to him with a tear rolling down her cheek. His words were truly unbelievable, something she never hoped to hear. He made her dream come true.

"What about the other women?"

"You go outside and have a view. See the forest. Have a bath in the river. If you enjoy you can go along with the women tomorrow morning." Adithya said and walked away with a proud smile.

But his attempts to turn a new leaf were foiled as he was called to his father's home and over there, his true instincts began to take over.

"It has been two days. Did you find anything?"

"Father, I need more time –"

"More time for this puny village? Plunder it! Take everything they have and move on, I say." Adithya felt physically hurt at his father's command. He looked at his father in shock, to which the old king replied, "Adithya... You are a ruler and don't forget that. Never forget who you are. A warrior whose very name strikes fear in all hearts. The one whose conquests will make history."

Adithya remembered a little boy carry a toy sword and playing in the royal palace, being told stories of heroic warriors who drew cold blood in the battle field. He idolised the soldiers in his army who had killed hundreds of people with their own hand. He recalled his childhood resolutions, "I will be the strongest fighter of them all."

"Adithya! Adithya – The Great! You have challenges to face, battles to fight, kingdoms to conquer and empires to rule. Your place is among the stars. You are a hero, don't forget that. Never forget who you are."

It wouldn't take more than 5 men to burn the village. He could kill every person in it, loot all their earnings and move on with another feather in his crown. Another story for the ballads to sing, another conquest for history to remember. He could march forward and establish his own empire with all the riches he had accumulated. An empire where he would be – God.

"Do what you love, isn't that what life is about?" Adithya loved to kill. He always loved the battle-field. Adithya was re-affirmed of his destiny.

"Stop!" Sita shouted at him and Adithya froze. She glided towards him and picked up a little squirrel from below his feet. "You almost hurt it", Sita picked it up and kissed the furry rodent.

Adithya drew his sword and pressed it against Sita's neck. But Sita's didn't even feel it. She stood up with the squirrel in her hand and a smile on her face that was directed at the prince. "Why are you smiling?"

"Why are you not?" The sword was on her neck, steadily held by him. Movement of a single muscle would splash her blood. But she still smiled. Adithya couldn't speak, noticing which Sita spoke up.

"Why are you not smiling? It is pretty easy you know."

"Yesterday morning also. I almost cut your head-off, but you didn't even flinch. Had I not stopped myself at that moment, you would be a dead person now. But you smiled."

"If you want to kill me, then I believe you have a very good reason to kill me. A very just reason to end my life. And my mother has taught me never to come in the way of justice. If you kill me, I will accept the death happily. I trust your judgement."

Sita could have pulled out her own dagger and stabbed him. She could have struck him from behind, she could have attacked him with her brothers' weapons, she could have sent her brothers and other villagers to attack him, or she could have at least cursed him for trying to take her life away. But instead, she stood with him, and that puzzled the prince. He could only fight an opponent, he could defeat a competitor, he could oppress a resistor. What could one do to a firm supporter? He knew that the king was waiting for him to act, and if Adithya did not declare war soon, the king would do that himself, and with people like Sita leading the village, it would spell disaster for the entire civilisation.

But why should Adithya be concerned. He always wanted the blood bath. What did the death of a few more people mean to him? What was the mystery that made him put his sword back?

That night he lay outside his house, gazing at the sky. "You are confused." Was that the sound of his conscience. Just as good. Sita walked from the aisle in between the fields to the thin strip of plain land that stretched a few feet outside Adithya's house.

"I am", he answered plainly having absolutely no intention of sharing his worries or doubts with her.

"And I can't help you?" Adithya nodded to her question.

Sita sat next to him cross-legged, putting her feet on her thighs. "Even I don't like lecturers and preachers. They never know the real difficulty. I am more of a do person. If I am ever confused about anything, I don't spend more than ten seconds thinking about it. Just do it." Adithya thought of slitting her throat. He grunted and turned away.

A breeze blew against Sita's face letting her hair fly in the night. There was a humming in the air, a slow buzz to which she listened carefully. Carefully she hummed along with the wind, catching up with its gentle rhythm and even pitch. As Adithya lay next to her, the frustration glowing on his face, Sita poured her soothing voice on it. The voice that brought everything to life, not just the forest but also the night.

Her song soon found listeners as frogs began croaking from the paddy field and bats glided across the sky. The moon smiled at her and the stars, as Das put it, came together to give shape to so many people and animals that eagerly listened to her song. But this time it wasn't just a melody that she sang, but a poem.

*The heart carries me to a distant land*
*Where neither I can sit, nor can I stand*
*Like the wind my heart goes on*
*It never stops —wandering all alone*

*It sways all along – here and there*
*Sometimes I fear, sometimes I care*
*What it searched for, I do not know*
*But I have to find out, there is no other go.*

*The wind sings a song, but I am too stubborn to listen*
*The voices in my head make it hard to take a decision*
*What is the mystery that holds me back?*
*What is the magic that makes me go back?*

*Questions are many, the wind goes on and on*
*But the answer is here, lying in a pond*
*The little frog that gives me company*
*I owe it much more than money*

*It makes me happy, it makes me proud*
*I give it my love, say it out loud*
*I think of again of my tryst with destiny*
*But the song gives me an epiphany*

*The breeze gives me a tickle, it soothes my darkness*
*Wherever, it serves that purpose*
*Share some joy, and some happiness*
*The frog and the wind – their hearts don't flicker*

The poem ended but Sita continued humming, with the frog and the wind to give it company. And the flickering heart that kept moving on, was touched by it all.

Adithya arose before the sun and went to his father's house as the first thing to do. "Father wake up!"
"What is it?"
"It is time. We have to prepare for battle."

# Chapter 6

## Love

He rushed over to the army camps and gave the commands to prepare for battle. It was not a battle cry, but an ambush. He talked to the army commander and told him to be ready with the all the horses and weapons and arrange special protection for the king and the women.

"What is going on?" His sister asked sleepily. As the prince looked at his sister's face, he froze for a second. Below her droopy eyes, there was a hidden smile, one that was gifted to her by her dear friend Sita.

"You never told me that it was so wonderful outside. So colourful and so bright. I walked with her for so long, I was afraid that my feet will break, but the air outside was so energetic – so powerful. And all the animals and plants and trees... and how she brought them all to laugh with her song. Such an amazing voice she has. Can you ask her to teach me to sing?" The stories of Adithi's venture didn't stop the previous evening as she narrated each and every sight outside the palanquin with eyes that had seen nothing else.

Adithya was reminded of Sita, the fervour with which she had shown him too, the forest. And the mention of her song made his heart beat faster. The memory of his previous night replayed itself in his mind.

The soldiers too were energetic, putting on their armour without any laziness or complacency that often infected them. "Must be something in the air. It is quite energizing." And it was Sita who injected the cheerful spirit into them. Soldiers who were born and raised amidst blood and death, whose heart had nearly turned into stone, who had little to claim human. The soldiers were savage beasts who worked heartlessly. But that morning even they wore smiles. "She always thinks about making people happy", Arundhathi's words echoed in his ears again. She does have a way of making people happy.

Adithya was indeed happy the previous night. Her song had lifted all the worries from his mind and brought a smile to his face too. He felt his heart as light as a feather, not flickering, but simply floating in the wind. Every sense of uneasiness was lifted off his head through her song, her voice seemed to wash everything away.

But then his wisdom and maturity took over. His father's word came in between and decided to fight anything that stopped Adithya from being the prince he was. He wanted to fight everything that stopped him from being a warrior. He decided that any further thought would create a bigger mess and followed Sita's last and only advice – Just do it. The prince decided to follow his instincts and reach his destiny.

"Adithya?" The army commander, Jayant, stared at him with sleepy eyes. "What?" Quickly bringing himself back from his pool of thoughts, Adithya asked. "I asked, when do we strike?" The commander repeated.

While the commander got irritated after asking just a couple of times, Sita sat next to Adithya for hours the previous night, singing songs and asking questions, or simply talking about something or the other in an attempt to lift his mood. That night she scurried off with a 'Good Night' only after ensuring that Adithya felt lighter at heart.

He turned around to check on the progress of the other soldiers. Behind the little huts that the soldiers lived in, Adithya could see that the vast forest was as still as crystal. His eyes could see absolutely no movement, as if there was no air at all over there. He thought of the spark Sita would have sent to the forest, shaking all the trees to life, like no other wind could. Every creature in the green paradise loved her voice. Even Adithya did. As his eyes moved from the forest another thought struck him, "What was I doing now?"

Oh! Checking on the soldiers. The absent mindedness irritated the prince but what agitated him more was that every time his mind slipped away, it dived into the thoughts of that dark beauty. She wore a simple robe, sometimes cream coloured and sometimes brown, and some simple jewellery made of pearls or wood. Her hair was tied behind her but even the lightest breeze would tear the knot and let her thick long hair flying. Her eyes shined on her dark face. And her dark skin was as beautiful as his horse.

She always carried herself like a feather, always so light. A contagious lightness that spread to everyone around her. Even at breakfast, whoever sat next to her couldn't stop laughing. The girls who accompanied her never stopped giggling and he had noticed many a times, how the little children in the village insisted on Sita's company for play. At the market she walked with a handful of children clinging on her feet and almost the same number resting on her shoulders.

Thus, everything Adithya saw, heard or touched reminded him of the girl who tried to make him happy. "What was the song again?" Adithya thought and tried to hum the words. But all he remembered was about a wind that never stopped and a frog that made her heart happy. Was she singing about him?

"Sir, all the soldiers are ready, where do we position them?"

"Wait, let the horses get ready too", Adithya commanded. "Where are the horses?"

One of the soldiers panted and told him, "Sir... they are not to be seen in the stable."

"What!?" Adithya was aghast! He rushed to the stable of his horses and found it clean and empty. "What are we waiting for? Let's go and search – Quick!"

Wearing a heavy armour and additional weaponry, the army spread to all four directions. Adithya too went in search, for one of the horses that went missing belonged to him. His horse was like a brother to him, upon which he rode since he was 9. With cold panic he ran through the forest looking for any sign of the Aryan beasts.

"Sir, I hear hooves", one of the men shouted and all the others ran towards the soldiers who was peeking through the overgrown grass towards the grass lands were a hundred naked horses galloped round and round with all the village children cheering at the top of their voices, some if it heard even in the forest from where they peeped.

Some of the horses were manned, some carried children and ran a little slower. Adithya eyes were quick to spot his Veera, running across the field carrying Sita on its bare back. His horse wore neither a saddle nor a bridle.

Adorned in his royal armour and carrying his Excalibur, Adithya descended from the forest and walked across the field, followed by his soldiers, towards his horse. He saw Sita get off the horse and let it gallop freely on the tall grass, faster than ever before. It took a wide circular jog and reached back to Sita as she kissed the horse on its forehead and brushed its hair with her hand.

Adithya walked all the way through the grassland to reach his horse, which brushed its head against the prince and Adithya patted its back in return. With great amazement and a lot of gratitude he said to Sita, "I have been riding it for the past fifteen years. And I have never seen it run so fast." He looked around to see the Aryan horses running side by side with the village horses, kicking up the adrenaline of all the viewers. "None of them!"

"I thought they were locked for too long so I decided to give them a little fresh air. Veera is such a strong horse!" Sita added in delight.

"Thank you", he said with a content smile and Sita smiled back.

Such a beautiful sight it was, more than a hundred horses galloping in the vast green grasslands as the sun slowly emerged from the horizon, carefully spraying its rays in the grass that reflected bright green. Their hooves shook the ground and whispered in the ear. Their pace energised anyone who saw the sight. The horses ran through the humans, and children of 4 and 5 screamed at the top of their voices as the animals ran past them, kicking up the dust and cutting through the grass. Even the grasslands came to life with Sita around.

"Sir?" one of the army men came up to him and asked.

"Get rid of your armour. Let's have breakfast."

Adithya decided to spend the rest of the day with his friends Anurag and Laxman. And he enjoyed saying that to himself – "Friends", "Friends", "Friends". He enjoyed spending time with them, like a teenager would while riding horses or playing tag with his friends. They joked and laughed about anything and everything; the two carpenters showed off their skill and Adithya tried to keep up by trying his hand with a few tools. That however, ended up in a disaster, nothing the resilient prince couldn't handle.

And for some strange reason, the memories and thoughts of Sita kept popping up in his head. The feel of a breeze, the touch of an animal, the sight of a scurrying ant, a crying child – everything led to his mind thinking about her. And every time she showed up, Adithya looked at her from the corner of his eye. The fickle minded prince' seemed to settle down on one thing at least.

Evening, when Anurag and Laxman called it a day, Adithya thought of accompanying the master magician of the village – the incredible Drupa. Nobody knows whether he chose to be with him because he was sure that Sita would be there too.

Consciously he avoided looking at Sita, but he couldn't help but turn towards her every now and then. And as often as he looked at her, so often did their eyes meet and Adithya awkwardly looked away. As the aroma filled the kitchen and took the tasters to the next world, as the taste buds danced on their tongues, Adithya just found another beautiful scene to associate Sita with.

That night when he lay under his thatched roof, Sita popped her head from the curtained window in his room and said, "Good Night". Adithya quickly got up and said, "Good Night". And Sita walked away, ruining a princely sleep.

She filled his dreams, dancing as elegantly as a swan, singing a song that poured a life into the forest that even the sun couldn't. She sat next to him and talked to him about horses and plants and trees and animals and music and dance and swimming and cooking and children and...

The next day again Adithya accompanied Laxman and Anurag, in an attempt to improve his skill. And the two were very patient with him, as a matter of fact, they even invited him to drop by the next day too even after an entire day had been wasted.

"Why can't I even get the hang of it?" Adithya complained.

"It is a rather herculean task. To carve things out of wood the way Laxman does. Even I can't do it like him. I only design the machines, he is the one makes them."

"Nobody can ever be as good as me. I am not being haughty, but just saying the truth. You will have to try things your own way if you have to be good at something. Do something different."

The amount of wood he had destroyed gave him a definite reason to sulk, and that in turn gave him a reason to talk to Sita. "I just can't seem to get it right."

"Nobody can do things like Laxman. Why don't you do something different?

"That is exactly what your brother told me."

"He is a very wise man."

"With a very abstract idea. What do you mean by 'something different'."

"You have to find that out yourself. That is the whole point. When you find out on your own, it makes the skill set unique to you. Don't worry, if you don't find something different, something different will find you."

"You are always optimistic."

"I know that's how the world works."

That night as Adithya carved Sita's face in the moon, she appeared behind him and said 'Good Night'. He answered, 'Good Night'. But before he could add anything else she was running back home.

That night he had colourful dreams. He dreamt of the thousands of millions of flowers that blossomed in the forest where Sita sang, of the so many different fruits that Drupa added to flavour his food and he laughed, in sleep, at how the pus of the fruit spilled out of the fruit and stuck to Adithya's royal clothes all day.

The next day he picked up a bunch of fruits and flowers from the forest, applied the sticky pus all over the little statues that Laxman made that day and applied the crushed fruit on the statues. How does this look? The young lady who was made out of black stone was given a fair skinned face and a golden red dress to wear. "NOW IT LOOKS LIFE LIKE!" Laxman exclaimed.

"This is something different!" Sita commented.

The whole day he spent colouring the various statues that Laxman made, using various fruits and flowers of so many different colours, and each statue earned thrice or four times the price that a normal one did.

"You can keep this, this belongs to you", Laxman gave Adithya three bags of rice and 8 yards of cloth that made up around three-fourths of what he earned.

"What am I going to do with all this?"

"You can use it yourself. Or you can trade it to buy something else you like."

"Can I have that little goat instead?" Adithya asked him pointing at a baby black goat that a customer had paid him for one of the statues.

"You can keep this one too."

"No, I need only the goat." Adithya carried the baby goat to his house along with a thousand instructions from Laxman on how to raise a goat.

That night he finished dinner early to attend to his new pet. Laxman had asked him to tie up the goat, But Adithya let the goat roam freely inside the house, just making sure by firmly shutting the doors and blocking his window that the goat remained in the house itself. He lay down listening to baby bleat. However, he couldn't fall asleep. Even after hours of laying down, he couldn't fall asleep. Adithya knew the reason very well.

He rushed out of his house, locking it firmly from outside and almost jogged towards Sita's house.

"Good night!" He said pushing his head through the window. Sita jerked awake and looked at him not being able to recognize the face in the dark with her sleepy eyes. She rubbed her eyes roughly and focussed at the neck that emerged from the square opening on her wall.

"Adithya!?" She exclaimed, her voice forgetting the time.

"You didn't... come to say good night today. So I came over."

"I did come over. But the doors and windows were shut." Adithya silently sighed in relief. For a moment he feared that she had forgotten the routine.

"Ohh... The goat... Just to keep it safe."

"Oh! How is the baby? Did you give it a name?"

"No, I didn't think of anything", Adithya said and stared blankly for a second. "Good night then", he said and pulled his head out of the window.

"Good Night" Sita shouted as he walked back to his house.

Adithya walked very slowly, keeping each foot ahead of the other after much consideration. There was something that pulled him towards Sita, a force that was nearly tangible. But he had no idea what it was. He thought of her all the time. He loved spending time with her. He found excuses to talk to her, had an urge to look at her but too shy to look at her in the eye. He had no clue as to what to talk to her, but prayed that they never stop talking.

Sita's wisdom had impressed Adithya on numerous occasions, and so had her courage. But the attraction he felt for her did not know reasons, it did not have logic. Adithya felt irrational and stupid. His father would have chopped him to death had he seen his son in such a pathetic situation. With hundreds of slave women to serve any pleasure he would want, why should he crave for the attention of some village girl? But he did crave her attention and presence... very dearly.

"Wait", Sita called out to him and made his heart leap. He turned around and saw her come out of her house, with her hair tied behind her neck and the ends of her hair let loose. "I will anyways wake up in another hour or so, and I don't think you are going to get any sleep either. Let's go to the river, shall we. I will show you my spot."

As he turned he felt the relief of having achieved his biggest ambition. With trembling hands and an over speeding heart he followed his... he followed Sita into the forest. The moon had become a thin strip and the forest they walked through was nearly impossible for Adithya to traverse and as he stumbled and tripped a dozen of times and almost fell on top of Sita, she said, "This is a pretty hard path. Hold my hand."

The hand which gripped a sword with unmatched firmness was ignorant of how to hold a woman's hand. But before he fumbled and messed up, Sita held him by his wrist and walked close to him along the narrow path. They finally emerged from the forest into the bank of the water which was as clear as glass.

The two of them sat on a rock near the river without speaking to each other. They listened carefully to the very slow flow of the river and the trickle of the water which splashed against a rock on the way. Adithya waited for her to catch up to the tune of the flow and start humming. But she didn't. Adithya didn't ask her to. Her silence was also musical for him.

Little things can change the world. A simple 'Good Night' or maybe a 'Wait', who knew that the sounds would reverberate for millennia to come? Who knew that the words would heal scars as deep as the heart?

Adithya was born a warrior, raised a warrior and he lived only to kill. His cup was always full, he never knew that something other than what he saw or what he heard existed. Women ruling the land, all humans living as equals, plants and animals being cared for, the river and the moonlight being cherished, all of that made him drop his sword. All of that was the mystery that held him back, that was the voice inside his head that said, "NO". And the knowledge that somebody cared for him, that a total stranger had the heart to be with him when he was torn, to say 'Wait' when he wanted to hear just that, he knew that the other world – the world of peace, love and happiness was where real life existed. To live in that world and share that paradise with somebody is the purpose of life. Adithya had become human.

At the riverside, listening to the silence of the water, seeing the darkness of the sky, he learnt what was hidden from him all along. And he loved the knowledge, he loved the person who taught him, he loved that land which enlightened him – his heart learned a new rhythm, his body found a new energy and his mind glowed with a light that filled every cell in his body. As he turned to look at the girl sitting beside him, the girl who sat next to him in the dark – just sat next to him, and he recalled all that she had been for him. She was the one who made him put the sword away again, she was the one who showed him the trees and the plants, she was the only one who told him 'Good Night'. Another wave passed through him, another pulse which added colours to every bit of him.

And those colours were bright, nothing like he had ever known. He could physically feel the love and affection, and she poured it to him endlessly. In that light he took an oath, that any honour that was left in him, any princely pride or glory that he ever earned or will earn, will be gifted to the girl who sat next to him in the night. For her presence gave him a joy that only three words could give – "I love you."

Sita always cared for everyone around her like no person could care for another. No matter whom she looked after, no matter whom she attended to, she poured all the love from her heart until it thoroughly exhausted her. She cared for people until it completely exhausted her mind and body, until it completely devastated her – the rejection.

Some say she asked for too much, some say she asked for only what she deserved and some others say that she only asked for what every person wants. To be loved by some person so much that he would lay his life down just for a smile to sprout on her face. Sita craved for that love, for that attention and care, and maybe that's why she poured out so much. Hoping that at least some of it will be repaid to her. Just hoping that some knight will save her from that castle of loneliness one day. That someone will drop by her house in the middle of the night to tell her a 'Good Night'.

And then she knew that her prince had come. In the darkness she could see the intensity of love in his eyes, the determination to care and love and the will to protect and hold on to her. That gesture told her everything she wanted to hear.

As he sat by her staring at nothing, listening to nothing, bearing the cold of the night, she knew that her heart filled up, that all the love that was exhausted had been put back in place with renewed energy. A new energy – the energy that only reciprocation could give. She felt the happiness that only five words could give – "Yes, I love you too."

The two of them sat by the river until the rustling leaves broke their silence. "My friends are coming it seems", Sita said.

Adithya looked at her and said, "I will see you", and walked away. No other words were exchanged. Strange, they had barely ever talked to each other, but seemed to read one another's mind. Strange!

They met at breakfast the next day, when Sita skipped her routine kitchen inspection to have a word with Adithya – "How are you?", "Are you feeling sleepy?", "Did you dance at the river today morning?", "Are you feeling hungry?"

At breakfast she quickly finished serving the food and sat along with the Aryans, right next to the prince. Later during the day Sita visited him at work and enquired about his paintings and which were selling like hot cakes in the village and in the evening before sunset Sita took him along with her on a raft through the river to visit all the five villages.

As the sun sank below the trees and the river turned from clear blue to a shade of red the two of them completed their tour and got back to the river bank where they had sat together all morning.

"I have some chores to attend to", Sita told him.

"Do you need any help?"

"No...", she said, thinking hard... how to tell him good-bye? How to stay with him for some more time. "I will meet you over here tomorrow. Early", said Adithya ending her dilemma.

"Laxman will come to bath here."

"Then you can come to my spot", he suggested and the love-birds bid adieu.

At night Adithya talked to his new friend, the little goat which Sita named Bitu, about their ride in the river. "She rowed the boat and talked endlessly – about the forest, the plants and trees and animals and birds and about the villages around them, their leaders, their people, their food; she told them how each village was different from the other yet they were all the same and lived like a single family, how all the villagers had love and respect for one another and always came to the others' rescue. She told me stories of her parents, their love affair, her grand-parents and great grand-parents. She told me the history of the civilisation, how science and art flourished over there and how the people developed into a society. And every time she pushed her raft through the water, she said about how wonderful and kind the river had been to them."

Adithya listened to her voice in rapt attention, not missing out a single word that was said. The chirping birds, the blowing wind, the flowing water, the rustling trees and the setting sun, none of it distracted him.

Sita lay in her house, but she found little sleep. Her mind was full of a new friend who had listened to her rambling all day. The magnificent trees in brilliant green, the clear water and the blue sky where thick white clouds were carved into immaculate shapes, thousands of birds and fishes all around them in so many colours and sizes and shapes, slicing through water and drifting through air, making you wish you have wings too – but all Adithya kept looking at was the girl who rowed the raft. Was she so beautiful? Sita never felt so, and she strongly believed that nothing could outdo the sights that their mother river had to offer. But Adithya, apparently, differed with her and a guilty pride made Sita smile.

"You make her very happy", Laxman told Adithya the next day. If Sita was his true love, Laxman happened to be his best friend, a relationship he celebrated just as much. "She is always happy, always cheerful, but I have known for a long time that there was some loneliness that haunted her. And I was never able to be with her. Thank you."

"There is little love I have known. I was educated by the wisest men of our nation and they taught me everything I needed to know, and I thought I did know everything – but your sister taught me the greatest lesson of all. To care, to share, to be with somebody. She has shown me something so wonderful... Beautiful! And I love her so much."

That day Sita entered her brother's workshop to find herself drenched in shock. Tears rolled out of her eyes and bathed her cheeks when she saw her statue standing in front of a wall... that had so many trees and flowers in it. In the middle a river flowed and the fishes danced with the swans in it. It front of it all, stealing the limelight from everything else, a dark girl swayed her hips to one side, joining her arms over her head and lifting one leg up almost as if she floated over the scenery. The picture of a beautiful Sita overshadowed the statue that stood in front of it. "It is still not as beautiful as the real you. It doesn't sing either", Adithya said as she got lost in the painting.

"A painting? Are you crazy?" The king roared at his son. Adithya's fame as a painter had rowed its way through the river to reach the entire civilisation, and the prince became another golden feather on the village's crown, a master who joined the elite gang of Anurag and Laxman. But little did his father acknowledge that.

"Have you seen them?" Adithya asked, genuinely hoping for an appreciation.

"I want to see a sword on your hands, not flowers. Red is the colour that you must wear Adithya!"

"Father, you do not understand."

"I see everything Adithya and it has to change. You will suffer, mark my words!" A remark that was clearly directed at another piece of news that had flown with the wind throughout the village – his affair with the celebrated dancing singer of the village.

"Perhaps it is only now that I don't suffer father. All along I have suffered, but only now I find peace. Only now I find love."

"This is going out of control. And now you are going to disperse the army?"

"Yes. They too are going to become a part of the village. Slowly they too must learn to accept this way of life."

"They are warriors! I will not let you destroy their honour and glory."

"There is not honour in killing. There is no glory in destruction."

"These are men who are feared by all."

"I want them to be men who are loved by all. I know what you are saying father, the soldiers are beasts. Ruthless beasts! They enjoy killing, they fight with no purpose, with no reason, with no heart. And this has to change. They must be shown the real world, the world of calm and peace."

The king's face had turned bloodshot red, "Our ancestors build this army. Our ancestors created these men. And I have spent an entire life winning the loyalty of these men and keeping them on my side. Even when the entire nation was divided, even when civil war broke out and the people rioted against us, when politicians and priests tried to oust us, I have kept the army intact. They are the strength of our clan. They are the key to our success, you cannot ruin them."

"Father you forget that they are humans too not killing machines! They need a life. They have never fallen in love – they have to."

"And it will not happen no matter how hard you try. The war is in their blood. They will never change. It is only a matter of days before they put on their armour on their own and unleash hell."

"Things will change father", Adithya said, for he had seen it with his own eyes. They were hungry for battle, but there was a shine on their face, a happiness in their

*Love*

voice that was unheard of. "They will change, they are changing —"

"Get out!" The king turned his face away and said. Adithya walked around his father to catch his eye but the king wouldn't let him have it. "A king's command will not be disobeyed. I will not let it happen. And if my own son chooses to disobey me, his punishment will be far worse."

The king spoke those words with conviction and Adithya knew that. He knew that there was a danger brewing up in the horizon, a storm waiting to break out. "I will be prepared." That evening he drew his sword out again but Sita was right behind him this time.

"Why are you holding it again?" Maybe for a second. Or a fraction of second there was a glitter in Adithya's eyes, one that the beast within him had whenever he held the sword. There was a small portion of his heart that still appreciated the beauty of the deadly master-piece. Just for a second.

"Nothing. I was... just making sure that we are prepared."

"Prepared for what?" Sita was deeply concerned. That sword had managed, very early in Adithya's life to split his personality into two and she very well knew that however deep it was, he loved the art of battle just as his painting. It was the most grave danger that Sita feared of.

But Adithya showed nothing of that and spoke like a man of sheer justice and logic, "The village is calm Sita. Everyone is in love and everyone is happy. But the village is not alone now."

"Your people are a part of us now."

"Even I have that hope. I have a lot of hope, most of all in you. You will change our men, you will make them real men. But I know very well what kind of threat they are."

"I will pray —"

"Prayers are simply not enough!" Adithya cut her short. He held Sita's hand and pleaded to her, "These are men who have seen nothing but their sword and shield all life. Red is the only colour they have seen, blood is the only aroma they know. Killing is their art, war is their religion. They are monsters!"

"Hush!"

"And I hope that they become human. I have faith that they will know of love and peace, but it is a risk."

"The sword is not a solution to anything Adithya, you have learnt that for yourself."

"A few months from now Sita, these men will learn our language. They will listen to us and understand what we speak. They will truly become one of us, but right now you have to admit that they are not."

"The sword will not heal any wounds."

"I know that, I know that, only love will... you have told me and I know that. But love will not stop a sword from slicing your neck off."

"Is it so?" Sita asked with a cunning look. How many times had her love stopped the sword at her neck from moving any further.

"You are not understanding Sita, they are not like me. They will kill. And I am afraid of what father has in his mind. We have to be prepared."

"Our village is always prepared Adithya. We are ready to face any disaster that may come our way. Our love will protect us, and all of us have faith. And I want you to have the same faith too. That faith is your strength. The sword is a coward's weapon."

"Nobody can convince you."

"Reason can convince me. Adithya, I know your fear, I know your concern. But let me tell you again, the sword will only add to injury. The sword can never save. Put it away."

With a sigh, Adithya tossed it away and it fell on the ground with a *clang*. Sita smiled at him and got up to go back home. Adithya stood up to see her off. She took two steps out of the house and rushed back to put her arms around him. Adithya held her tightly in his arms. Only the clouds witnessed the two of them become one. Only the clouds and a little goat.

# Chapter 7

# Ahimsa

The sun had risen from the sky but it did not bring along the celebration its glow always carried. And most of the older people in the village acknowledged the silence and calm with a sigh of relief.

"So nice this silence is. Only now I realize the kind of havoc that is being wrecked every morning in our village. But what happened today morning? Are any of the children not feeling well?" One of the elderly men, the previous leader of the village asked his fellow elders while sitting under a tree outside their homes, having their usual morning gossip.

"Not to my knowledge, no. But I can't see any of them outside. Wonder why?" The other old man observed the street outside his house that morning and smiled at the emptiness. The grass was visible on the ground, a really new sight as the green earth was always under the little feet of children who spilled across the village, playing all day. Or there would be travellers or traders moving around, the village ladies going around for a stroll, the village men building another road or widening an existing one, some young girls planting a new tree if any spot was left out, even if it was just big enough to hold a single seed or at least the young men of the village would be seen showing off their exploits, maybe a new invention or a statue or a painting.

Even Drupa's house had breakfast in silence and only the Aryans had come to have a bite off the master-chef. And the Aryan soldiers too ate in complete silence. "Very odd", the entire family of Sita, her parents and her brother said in unison.

"What is going on?" Adithya reached the house that morning after having breakfast at his own house.

"Nothing much actually. Nothing at all, not even a breeze", unlike the old people, the younger villagers did not enjoy the absolute silence. Even Sita felt the silence had an eerie air to it than one of peace and calm. "She did not sing anything today morning!" Malati had complained at their bath.

"Why didn't you have breakfast with us today morning?" Arundhathi snapped at Adithya.

"I have burdened you people long enough. My food may not taste anywhere as good as Drupa, but I have to live with it. My own food."

"Rubbish Adithya. What else are we here for. And you are no stranger either." The village leader complained.

"I will certainly have one meal over here, everyday. But not all meals, not when I can feed myself. By the way how are the supplies coming? There seemed to be some shortage."

Adithya had picked up the pulse of the village and understood matters like trade and economy even better than Sita did. Arundhathi's face turned a little serious and but she smiled it away and said, "Why do you worry of such matter when I am here?"

"Because I am the cause of your worry. And my people. They eat all day without any payment, without doing any work. I do realise that we have over-stayed our welcome."

"Adithya, don't be stupid", she chided him.

"I have been asking them to find some work. But as I have told you before, it is rather hard for them to... adjust. This new kind of life. Some of them were celebrated heroes of their times in their lands. They find it hard to do any other work." Adithya added after a pause, "other than killing."

"Adithya! I thought I was the one who was supposed to take care of that. You just mind your own business, go to work", Sita intervened.

"Hey, speaking of work. Where is Laxman?" News was still rather slow to reach him in the village.

"He was roaming around with Das for the past couple of days. Didn't even come home for a couple of nights. Reached home today morning just before sunrise and went to sleep."

Adithya looked around and felt uneasy, "Maybe it's because he isn't around, Laxman. Feels odd. Uneasy." Sita went beside him and held his hand but did not say anything. The silence was disturbing and as much as she wanted to, she couldn't console her prince.

And screaming his lungs out, as if to reverse any damage the silence might have done, the eccentric Das reached the house of the village leader that afternoon just as preparations for lunch was going on. Laxman had just woken up and looked at his best friend with fearful eyes, un-believing eyes. Arundhathi and Sita too emerged and brought Das to sit down and tell them what had happened. But through his gasps and panting, nothing made sense. Finally he calmed down and said, looking at Laxman in the eye, "I was right. We have to leave!"

"No!"

"What's going on!?" Sita exclaimed. Das' unusual behaviour was nothing to be amazed about, but her brother's reaction was scary. There was an urgency and tension in both their voices. "What is going on?" she asked again.

"We have to leave! Get our personal supplies ready and send someone to spread the words right away. Ask some to go to the other villages too and give them a warning. Sorry Sita, but I don't think we have the time to tell you everything."

"But what am I supposed to do if you don't even tell me what is going on?" Sita held her brothers' hand and he got irritated.

"You go ahead Laxman, I will tell them everything", Das said and Laxman rushed off.

"Where is he going?" Arundhathi asked, losing her patience.

"To find Anurag and Adithya. We have to escape. There is a flood coming!"

"What!?" Arundhathi and Sita exclaimed in unison. As they stared at Das, he sat up and began narrating his story, the urgency all the more evident in his voice as he sat up and his arms trembled.

"Not just the stars, but I have also been noticing the clouds, the shapes they wear, how they move, how it rains, and how the wind blows. I had been at the task for such a long time that I was very thorough with all the patterns in the sky. I was able to predict and time and amount of rains we would be receiving, weeks in advance.

"And a few weeks earlier, I made a very peculiar calculation. The wind will blow faster than anything you have ever, according to my calculations, carrying with it anything that came in the way. And rains that would make our mother river puke. Thunder and lightning that will burn the forest. All our homes will be wiped out in the storm, everything will be destroyed, everyone will die!"

The two women were completely silenced by his words. Their hands trembled as he spoke of their imminent death. "I couldn't believe myself either. I checked and rechecked my calculations, but the sky kept repeating itself to me. Then I had Laxman cross-check my calculations. I was sure that I had made some mistake, but no! And now there is little time."

"How little?" Arundhathi asked with stuttering words.

"Less than a week."

"A week..." Arundhathi analysed her plan of action, but Das cut her short, "but the problem is... there is nowhere to go. We cannot escape, the storm is going to be really huge. We cannot survive it."

Arundhathi's nearly collapsed when out of the corner of her eyes she saw her son run towards her along with Anurag and Adithya. Anurag quickly reached for Das and asked, "How long did you say we have?"

"A week. Definitely not more than that."

"We can run. Move from the village, go somewhere far off."

"It is not possible", Das cried.

"It is possible actually, but too dangerous. We are surrounded by the river on one side and a desert on the other. According to Das the entire river will overflow, wiping us off, so that is not an option. And if we choose to go through the desert then I don't think we will be able to return alive. The blazing heat will eat us up, there is no way we can carry enough supplies to keep us alive for that much time. We have to stay here and fight the storm", Anurag said. As he paused and as Arundhathi searched the faces of the other men, begging for a way out, Adithya pointed to Anurag and said, "He has an idea."

"How strong did you say the winds were?" Anurag asked.

"Strong enough to blow away our houses."

"The trees? The trees in the forest, will they fall?"

Das thought for a moment and shook his head, "No, they won't fall. The really old ones... I am not so sure, but most of the other trees are strong. They will stand the wind."

Anurag looked at Laxman and Laxman nodded in understanding. Arundhathi shouted at them impatiently, "What do you have in mind, will you please speak up?"

"Tree-houses", Laxman said to all of them. "It was a very old design Anurag made. To build houses on trees just like birds build nests. But then we dropped it when we thought it would harm the birds and the forest at large. But right now it seems like a good options."

"And the birds?" Sita enquired.

"They have all escaped. Didn't you notice the silence this morning?" Das affirmed.

"But Das says that the wind will be strong enough to blow away houses. Then how will a tree house help, is it not a similar design after all? Even weaker if you ask me."

"The trees will slow down the wind. Still the design needs to be changed. Laxman, can you arrange for the wood in the mean time? Same old measurements."

"It will be ready right away."

"Das can come with me to my workshop and help me design the tree-house. I want to know how fast the wind will be and how strong the trees are. Sita, can you bring Malati to me?"

"Right away", she said and dashed away.

"Adithya, shall we get to work?"

"I am still not good at wood, you know that", Adithya said helplessly.

"You will not be carving any wood, just cutting it in the right measurements. And if we don't have enough wood, we will have to bring some from the forest. Can you ask you friends to help? More the hands the better."

"I will ask them to get ready", Adithya said without a moment's hesitation.

"I will spread the word and ask everybody to be prepared", Arundhathi said and walked back into the house. She turned to her children from inside the house and added, "Be calm and don't let the others panic", she said and set off to work.

Within minutes the sleepy village transformed into a buzz of activity with Arundhathi in the epicentre managing the mob. While her son worked without break to arrange the wood along with Adithya and his soldiers, some of whom Adithya managed to convince and employ to work, her daughter assisted the young men and Anurag with whatever they needed and her husband assembled the people around him and did his best to calm them down, preaching them from the bottom of his heart first and if that didn't work – feeding them, Arundhathi redressed the villagers' problems and concerns. "Where will we go if all the houses are destroyed?", "What about my children, they are barely old enough to walk?", "What about my parents, they are too old to even stand?", "What about all the valuables like the statues your son made?", "What will we do for food?", Arundhathi attended to all the queries with all her breath trying to convince them with calm reply for the moment and at the same time making sure that the problems they raised were addressed to by someone or the other. She arranged for all the food and the workforce that she could assemble and put them to one work or the other.

Some helped Laxman arrange the wood, some helped pack up the necessary food and a bunch of villagers along with Malati set off to the forest to identify the old trees, to collect some wood and to mark the really strong trees which would support their tree house.

At night all the wood had been made ready and Anurag was ready with his final design for the tree-house. "Das expects the water to reach as high as 3 men tall", Anurag began to explain, "So we will have to build the tree-houses around 5 men tall. There won't be a proper roof but just planks of wood that are laid across the forest at that height. This is because, that plain structure will be the easiest and strongest that we can build in such short time. Also a roof could be risky if the wind cuts through and blows it off.

"We are providing some space for the rain water to flow away and there will be a number of rafts for our immediate need. All of us will have to reach the planks before the storm starts - starting with the toddlers and the old men.

"Das also told me that there might be a forest fire, in which case we are all dead. But since the trees are really tall, it will take in any lightning that may strike, and since there will be heavy rains, the fire will be extinguished soon. So I guess we will start building right away."

Men and women climbed the young trees marked by Malati carrying the wood on their backs and little by little, carried all the wood to 5-men height on the trees. All night they spent fixing the wood onto the trees, each end of the plank being fixed at the same level to ensure even height.

Within two days all the planks were ready and strong enough to carry all the people of the village, so the villagers started to carry the older people and the toddlers to the planks along with their care-takers. The older people included the Aryan king and his ministers who were the among the first set of elders to ensure their safety. As villagers began climbing onto the plank, the wind began to blow at a normal, yet scary pace. The blow had a nasty voice.

Within three days all the village citizens had relocated themselves to the tree-top planks that stretched itself across the forest, as vast a paddy field. The wind gathered strength and whistled throughout the forest. Mothers and father looked across the forest anxiously.

And just as Anurag had predicted, the storm came – nastier than anyone could imagine. "Hold on to something", Laxman announced and everyone hugged a tree near them. Families stuck to each other as close as they could, holding one another as tightly as possible. The villagers also managed to bring some of the smaller pets to the planks, but the cows and horses could only be left on their own. Children cried profusely at the thought of losing their dear cows, of sacrificing their dearest horses, but all knew that nothing could be done, except hope, that the animals can fend for themselves. The animals had become such a close part of each family.

The men saw with horror, through the huge branches of trees, the sights that unfolded in the village. Water poured over the houses, flushing through the streets from the river and wiping clean off anything that stood in its way.

For a while the trees could give them shelter but soon water started dripping onto their planks and the wind cut through the forest to find the hidden human population. Some of them tried to protect themselves by holding themselves under huge leaves and standing under a protruding plank of wood but none of them stayed dry for long. Thankfully, Anurag's design allowed the water to flow through the planks and this was the least comfort they had.

Sita held on to her family, putting her arms around Drupa and Arundhathi, and Laxman put his arms around all three, holding with the tip of his hands the branch of one tree. Toddlers cried their eyes out as the endless darkness was suffocating.

Lightning struck over the sky, informing the world of its arrival through the boom of a thunder. Everybody looked up at the sound of the thunder and prayed in silence.

For 3 days they couldn't bath properly or even eat properly. Much of the supplies they had brought were washed away and each family held very little food that could barely support them through the storm. A number of villagers turned cold in the water and weren't able to move. All of them lost their energy.

And finally when the buzz in the forest ended, one of the village men decided to climb down and see if the storm had finally ended. He carefully treaded his way towards the village along with a few other men including Drupa and Laxman and saw just what the expected, the flood had washed their village into a barren land which had nothing. There was no sign that a civilisation ever existed on that land. The roads, houses, grasslands, agriculture fields, trees planted by them – all of it was mercilessly washed away by their mother. Not a single building survived.

"The flood is over. Everything is over", Laxman climbed up to the plank and informed them that it was safe to get back.

"What will we do for food?" One of the villagers enquired.

"We will just go and see how the other villages managed to survive. For the time being we will have to depend on our forest for food", Arundhathi announced, her voice did its best to dispel some of the concerns of the people.

"Can we hunt for food?" Adithya asked. Arundhathi turned to him and said, "If forest fruits do not suffice then we will have to hunt, we have no other choice. My grandparents used to hunt very frequently, but the younger generations don't fancy meat. Sita will probably hunt you down before you try to get some animal", the efforts to bring a cheer was evident from her voice. She tried to laugh away the sentiments of the loss she had suffered. Only in the evening did they, however, understand the true magnitude of their loss.

"Nobody survived. The other four villages are completely washed off", one of the messengers announced with a sob and the news stabbed everyone on the chest. Village people of all ages, including Adithya mourned the loss. All of them cried, their tears were more devastating than the flood itself.

"We have to look ahead. No use in crying now. Let us rebuild." Somebody said. That night itself all the crying stopped. Friends, relatives, pets, homes, workplaces and a lot more was lost, Some of it couldn't be brought back but the village people resolved that whatever could be brought back – "We will bring it back!"

"For so long I was afraid to strike, afraid that I might be killing the duck that laid golden eggs." As the night was young and the exhausted village fell asleep, the king called his trusted commander and said, "This was a good place to stay, a nice place to rest, good food, good hospitality, but I feel we have over-stayed our holiday. It is time to get to work."

"As you command, your highness."

"Make all arrangements for battle. We will be taking all the people slave for our next journey. Before the full moon shows itself, every man and woman who sleeps in this land must proclaim me as their supreme king and bow down to me. God has sent this flood just for me. Now I will recreate the village as I desire. The first thing to build will be palace for me, right in the centre of the village. And then I will send people in four directions to look for other nations in the neighbourhood. With this plentiful paradise as home, I will rebuild my empire.

"The first thing I need for that is my son. I want my son back. Tomorrow night I want the girl and her family dead. And if somebody tries to stop you, unleash hell upon the village."

The sun emerged from the sky stirring up a tide of activity. Putting the past behind them and taking a vow to build a beautiful future, the resilient citizens got off to work with unbelievable vigour. And leading re-construction like a true leader from the front, Arundhathi took command and set the wheel in motion. All the youngsters were split into teams and sent for various tasks, one of them set off to the forest to collect as many fruits and other eatables as possible, with Malati leading the troops, while another was sent in the opposite direction to look for stone and wood, led by Laxman. Anurag and Das were in-charge of designing the new city – one that would be an improvement of all the drawbacks that their old village faced. Roads had to be wider and smoother, more houses needed to be constructed and the forest area too had to increased, a decision the village took as a show of thanks, for the forest had saved their lives and continued to support them at the time of crisis. Instead of having separate workshops for different people, it was decided to have a fewer number of workshops that were larger and would accommodate more number of people. And all the agriculture land was to be shifted to the outskirts of the village, closer to the other villages and possibly even beyond the forests so that it would provide them with some ease of transportation.

Drupa led another bunch of men and women to take care of those who were sick and tired and needed care, something he always did from his heart. Drupa took the older men, who had lost their children who migrated to the neighbouring villages, in his hands and comforted them warmly. And that job required a lot of stamina because he himself was shattered. His home, his kitchen, his pets, his way of life, his routine – everything was turned upside down and being a man who placed his emotions higher than anything else, the pain inflicted by the flood was too severe. But when an old woman mourned the untimely death of her grandchild, Drupa could only hold back his tears and placing a comforting arm on her shoulders.

Bitu, Adithya's baby goat too was taken away by the flood. As soon as water had cleared, he walked over to the land where his house once stood and searched around for the animal, hoping it would have somehow managed to escape. Just praying that it was safe. He could have carried the animal to the planks on top but when he noticed that there would be a possible constrain in space and lack of supplies, and when all the villagers decided to leave the animals for themselves, with a heavy heart he hoped that his pet would survive. The animal that he had raised like a son was no more. He had just started to love and care, and the world put his emotions to the test.

But the villagers had vowed to move forward and he went along with them. He would build the village again, his village, his home. He spent the entire day in the forest with Laxman and reached their erstwhile village only after the sun had set, to report to Arundhathi of their progress and how much further time they would require.

That evening all of them discussed on how to move forward, building a dream-world that was to become the foundation on which their new village would be built. As Laxman showed them all the wood and stone he had manage to collect, and Malati brought home enough food for the village, the sense of optimism that had dwindled for a moment was re-ignited and pumped into the hearts of all. And when the energy reached its peak, the air bore a different taste that brought a tune to Sita's lips. Amidst the cheers and joy, Sita set off into a musical and the village relished her voice which made them forget everything else.

"Adithya, there is something important", one of the Aryan soldiers tapped his shoulder and called him. Reluctantly he stepped aside to talk with his men. But before they could start he recollected his thoughts and demanded angrily, "What were you people doing all day? I will not have so many men sitting idle as the village is in crisis."

"That is what we called you for, my prince. We were called by the king", one of the soldiers told Adithya. He sensed the doubts and questions the prince would shoot at him and continued, "The king is going to attack the village and take its people slave. The battle will start today, we will strike the leader's home. We have very strict commands that no matter what happens, Sita and her family will die tonight", he said the last words in a grave tone.

And Adithya listened to them with fear creeping out of the depths of his heart and showing itself on his skin. "The village gave him food and shelter and now it has saved his life from the flood. But the king wants to kill them in return? I have to talk to him", Adithya said and marched towards his father but the soldiers stopped him.

"The command has been issued and the soldiers are ready to fight. A hundred and fifty fighters have been stationed at different corners of the forest and they will strike one by one. There is nothing you can do now." He listened to the words in utter disbelief. He had been through a disaster and managed to save an entire village and just as life was getting back to normal...

"All of us were instructed to take our weapons and be ready to attack. 'Kill anyone who doesn't bow', that is our command. And then our commander said that our first target was to be Sita and her family. That, we could not do. Drupa is a man who has fed us for so many days, no we cannot kill him. And his daughter, no, we couldn't even think of hurting her. We split-up from our battalion and reached you."

"How many of you?" Adithya asked nervously. "Please don't be less than ten!" he prayed.

"Around thirty of us", quickly his mind went on to calculate the war strategy. Thirty of them fighting against a hundred and twenty was a very much winnable battle.

"Let's get to work", Adithya said and marched along to reach his loyal men. Thirty of them greeted the arrival of the prince with relief. He looked at them confidently and spoke.

Sita lay on the ground staring at the sky, the moon had a little chunk taken out of it. There were deaths, there was loss, there was a disaster and it was a tragedy, but Sita's sense of happiness did not diminish. Her hope was strong and although nothing could make up for the lives that were lost, she knew very well that the sadness caused by such loss could easily disappear. There was a brand new future to look forward to and Sita found it somehow, much brighter than her past. She looked around her to find all the villagers asleep in the common ground and searched for Adithya. She had noticed him disappear during her song and he hadn't returned yet. She was sure he would tell her 'Good Night' before he slept.

Her thoughts drifted from the ideas and visions she had for their new village to the new home they would build for herself and Adithya. They could buy another baby goat and a couple of other pets too. They would go to bath together every morning, she would sing songs exclusively for him and he would paint for her. She dreamt on about their children and the moonlight was blocked by the shadow of a man. She sat up to see a strange dark armoured figure holding a sword over her head. She simply sat there looking at him as the man took one step forward and swung his sword at her.

But that too did not reach her body, another sword pierced his body from behind and the dark man dropped his sword and fell dead on the ground. Behind him, Adithya stood tall with a bloodied sword on his hands.

"Come on, get up! We have to run!" He grabbed Sita by her hand and dashed into the forest, away from the common ground where all the villagers slept together. When the darkness around them became absolute and they reached the thickest part of the forest, Sita made the prince stopped at her tracks. "What is going on?"

she screamed. A voice that the forest was very familiar with, but not the tone.

"It is an ambush. I am taking you somewhere safe until things settle down."

"What do you mean settle down?"

"You need not know Sita. Just be safe!"

"Adithya, I am not moving anywhere unless you put that sword away."

"I have no time to argue with you. If you aren't coming along then I will have to carry you all the way." Adithya tried to grab her but she slipped out of his hands.

"Please", Sita begged, "please put it away."

"SITA, THEY ARE GOING TO KILL YOU!" Adithya shouted. "My father has given his command. The soldiers are going to take over the village and as a first step they are going to kill you. Before full moon the entire village will be under his foot, all the men and women will become his slaves, his subjects.

"And using this village as his home, he will spread out his terror to all the neighbouring lands. If he is not stopped now, he will be stopped never!"

"The sword may kill a terrorist. But it will never kill terrorism!" Sita spoke in a calm voice and she wanted to inflict the peace upon him. "Your father will understand. If you could understand, then your father will definitely understand."

"There is no point in convincing him now. There are a hundred and fifty monsters around us vying to kill us. Monsters who won't listen, who will not learn. Once they have started to kill, they cannot be stopped. They have been trained that way."

"We will stop them."

"I have told you Sita, time and again, IT IS NOT POSSIBLE TONIGHT", he shouted angrily, his face turning red and hot. "The war is today, and the killer is right behind you with his sword at the ready. Only a shield or another sword can stop him. We do not have the time to touch their hearts and change their minds. What is important to me right now is your life."

"I don't want to live Adithya. If my life means the death of so many people then what is the purpose of my life. Please let me die…"

"Is that all I mean to you? Do you think you can leave me and die so easily?"

"Adithya. Your decision will echo for millennia to come. You have to choose what precedent you wish to set. Do you want our children to choose a sword?"

"For love – Yes!"

*Crack*

A twig broke on the ground and swords slashed against each other in the darkness. Adithya held Sita firmly by his side and chopped off the other swordsman by his leg. He moaned and fell to the ground.

Suddenly the forest went ablaze and the fire showed him a dozen of warriors around him, waiting to pounce. And one by one they jumped at him.

Adithya blocked the swords that were aimed at him from three sides and kicked them away one by one and instead of blocking the fourth sword he moved away and chopped of the arm that held the sword. Before the other's raised their swords, Adithya let go of Sita for a moment and leaped at them. He dodged the sword that came his way and pressed his own sword at the enemies heart, pulled it out and sliced the neck of another man who had raised his weapon at the prince.

He grabbed another sword from one of the soldiers and slashed it at two men simultaneously who managed to block it the first time but felt it go through their neck when he waved it again.

Sita couldn't believe her eyes, how masterfully Adithya tore apart twelve warriors before the fourth blink of her eyes. The prince stood before him with blood splashed all over his body, his posture wearing the pride of victory and his face wearing the honour of murder. Sita ran towards him and hugged him tightly. "Please, no more Adithya, no more. You cannot kill more men, they too have… families and happiness… and pain. You cannot do this, please don't do this." Tears ran out of her eyes when she looked at the sights around her. Men – armless, headless and some even heartless. The gore made her puke.

"I am sorry you had to see the bloodbath. I promise Sita, no more. I just want one more night. I swear to you that after tomorrow morning, I will never hold my sword again. I will not hurt anyone, please give me one night. One last night."

"It will not end Adithya, please understand. They will keep coming to attack us, everyday for the rest of our lives. You have to end this now, right now!"

"I will not give up your life or mine simply at the hands of a tyrant. I will not give up" Adithya said and gently pushed her apart. Sita fell to the ground crying. Adithya reached to Sita to pick her up when suddenly another sword came and zipped past him. The prince picked up his sword but the other soldier was running away in fear. Adithya took four long strides and pounced upon him with his sword cutting through his head. As he turned around he saw another one of the men slashing Sita's backbone.

Adithya dived to catch Sita before her blood touched the ground. He felt the cut in her back and with bloodshot red eyes, hoping it only tore the skin, understood that the injury had cut her vertebrae. The sword was waved at him one more time but he held the man by his hand and pressed it so tightly that he dropped the sword and cried in pain. Adithya grabbed the sword and slashed his head, which got separated from the body and fell on the ground.

He held the lifeless body of Sita close to his chest and screamed out the very last drop of air from within him.

# Book III

# Chapter 8

## Return

"Dev!" Once again I was back at my very own office, the very same desk which instilled within me the desire to excel. And apparently I did excel. After my work with Kanha I was given 2 assignments one after the other with absolutely no time to rest. So this time around when I was back at my seat there was a sense of relief coupled with the nostalgia of my days before and after the idle time.

Before the idle time was my human life and I recalled my last days as I played with my six year old grand-daughter, the apple of my eye. Until my last day I have attended to her every need, from waking her up to brushing her up to dressing her up, all the way to playing with her and doing her homework too. And the naughty girl too was adamant that I, and only I take care of her. I peeked through the Haven portal and saw her looking after her own child and telling her daughter stories that I had told her. "She still remembers!" I thought excitedly.

As I strolled back from the Haven Portal back to my seat, I recalled the way I had walked those steps for the first time. I didn't – I was thrown out of the window.

Spending so much time with my grand-kid had to a certain extent turned me too into a kid and in my afterlife too I had taken the shape of a fairly young boy – many said I looked around 14-15. And that really helped me enjoy my work with the legendary Kanha.

That was one experience I dearly enjoyed, because as a conscience Kanha was such a unique learning experience. I mean, when you think of a nerd you feel they are so obedient and all that, but even for a person like Kanha who was obsessed with obedience, the task of a conscience was challenging. Challenging unlike any other task I had taken up after that. Happily I recalled the moments I had spent with Kanha – 17 blissful years they were! After that I had taken up 2 assignments of 3 years each, both Chartered Accountants. It was truly awesome except for the fact that they were drastically hopeless when it came to communication skills. How do you expect them to listen to their conscience when they don't listen to their own personal secretaries?

The first few days of peace – I loved it, but then you know how it is; even the laziest of all can't sit idle for more than that and I started pestering my manager all over again, "Next assignment?", "Next assignment?" and the crafty gentle-soul would give me his usual laugh and cracked one of those stale jokes which made no one laugh.

Finally the boredom reached a fever pitch and I told him, "Praveen, I am going to take a look on Kanha. Just check out what he is doing, it has been a long time. And now that I am free, no issues right?"

"Nah… just make sure his current conscience doesn't get pissed off. I mean, he shouldn't feel that someone else his supervising him."

"No, no… I am just going to check up on him. He must be around 23 years old right now, huh?"

"I guess. Go see for yourself. Don't make it too long a visit and you are not supposed to talk to him."

"Been at the job for quite a while now, I know the basics." Praveen - the manager's childish advises irritated me, or rather, insulted me. But I was too deep in a nostalgic ocean to think about anything else. I looked up Kanha's old files that I had prepared and recollected the boy.

His height was sort of average for his age and had a lean body with barely any muscles or bone strength to show off. His head was shaped exactly like his father's, a perfect cuboid but every other feature was inherited from his mother, he pretty, large eyes, slender nose hairy forehead, thin ears and well shaped eyebrows, everything somehow suited the cuboidal face wonderfully well.

He was studious, obsessed with obedience, quite selfish and wanted to change the world. He did not treasure his friends all though he did have an angel for a friend. He had a wild crush on some pretty face, completely lost his ways in her heart and then had one heck of a recovery towards the end of his twelfth grade, and I have not even found out what happened to his results.

I wondered how his body was doing, and how the internal politics settled down inside him. Was he physically fitter? Had his skin tone reduced? Did he suffer any injuries? Where they all united? I kept my fingers crossed when I wished that, "I hope his brain is still in charge." I made a self note saying that the first thing I would do on reaching Kanha was to ensure that he was healthy and fit and did regular exercise and all his cells were happy. He was planning to do a CA, I recalled... Ooops! I slapped my head and cried, "Not another CA!"

Just as I was about to step into the portal and head towards his home, a colleague emerged out of it and I immediately recognised him and Kanha's present conscience. "I can't take him anymore. Please give me some other human and let someone else handle the situation. I am helpless."

Praveen and I looked up at him with a grave look and the frustrated conscience explained, "He tried to commit suicide."

Praveen looked at me quickly as I jumped off the Haven Portal to reach my very first client, my dearest Kanha. 23 years back he had thrown me off the window to reach him and this time too I emerged through the clouds in the same pace to reach the very same hospital, on my own volition.

I entered the hospital and saw him lying on the bed being attended to by a couple of nurses. They seemed to be relaxed and the doctor had told them, I heard them think, that he was never even in a dangerous position. He might have been if he was not rescued on time.

He was unconscious and I went inside his body to find out that only the essential organs worked calmly. Some of the cells recognised my and happily greeted my visit. I had thought of asking them what was going on but felt it better to talk to the brain directly. The heart however mentioned as a passing remark, "Don't know what is wrong with him, but for the past few years he seems really upset. He has no reason to be so, if you ask me, but he simply is upset."

"Hmm... let me investigate and find out then."

"Oh! So you are back as his conscience huh?"

"I guess I am. I have to get a confirmation from Praveen. You guys take rest, I will be back when he wakes up."

"Be back soon. Nobody can sort out a crisis better than you can", I couldn't say how sarcastic the heart was in his comment but I do recall that my chest had got pumped up.

I slipped out of Kanha's body after ensuring that there was no mortal danger to him and made my way all the way back to my office to meet Praveen. "It is official right?"

"It is a policy of our firm and my personal wont that a conscience must not guide the same human for such a long period of time. But your job got registered automatically and now you will have to serve as his conscience for another one year at least", Praveen sounded as if he had been cheated.

"That's awesome", I completely ignored his tone and celebrated the fact that I was getting back to my best buddy. You won't understand. It is always much more interesting to guide a youngster, especially someone like Kanha, than to go along with an old man. The youngsters fall into all kinds of troubles and then listen to us, keeps our job sort of interesting. "First I would like to meet all the conscience souls who had served him during the past 6 years. Can I have the list?"

Praveen gave me a list of all the souls who had worked as his conscience and I was stunned to find 9 names in the list including my own. And none of them had completed the mandatory period of one year. I felt that really odd and intriguing so I went about to meet them one by one to compile the past of Kanha from 17-23. Six years of his boring life looked somewhat like this:-

"Kanha cleared his 12th standard examination with exactly 95%, just as he had hoped for", my face lit up, "and right away he wrote his CA-CPT examination which also he cleared with distinction. The gloom that existed in his house during his 11th and 12th standard had disappeared and Kanha once again became a teacher's pet and the 'apple of my eye' for his parents. After the crisis of his 12th boards, Kanha was very careful about his body and put serious effort into keeping himself fit with a proper diet, adequate exercise and good sleep. Kanha went on to prepare for his CA-IPCC exams where he put an intense effort and spent all nine months dedicating himself for that purpose, reflecting in his approach the child he had been.

"All said, he still had difficulty in making friends or keeping friends and none of his acquaintances appreciated the trait he carried. He put his goals ahead of everything else and cared little for anything else." Oh, this fellow rhymes too. "And that was the only thing that his conscience, I, requested him. I consistently advised him that he was not the only human in the world and he won't be able to survive on his own but Kanha never paid heed to his guides' words.

"Sometime around his IPCC exams a sort of depression began to creep into his brain. His body worked smoothly and Kanha had the Midas touch in everything he did, securing a good All India Rank for his IPCC exams, but the gloom continued to haunt him." And I think I know what the reason is.

"Kanha convinced his parents that Chennai was the proper place for him to do his 3 years of articleship and thus set off to the South Indian Metro, where he lived in a flat with two friends and found that the loneliness began to pain him. His parents had always cushioned him from being lonely and gave a proper structure to his life. His parents kept his emotional quotient on check and without their presence around him, Kanha's depression began to take a toll on him.

"But as his conscience I very well knew that loneliness was only a reason that magnified his depression and the real source of his pain was something unknown to me. I conveyed the matter to Praveen and told me that such emotional troughs are normal and it would heal itself in time. It did not and I have to admit that working with a man of such a dark heart is a truly suffocating experience.

"Office was a fun place to be and it very often inspired him and sometimes even lifted his spirits but as exam pressure became imminent and studies took a priority, Kanha's depression only turned worse.

"None of it affected his body or his social stature. Kanha was a very respectable person, admired by many but loved by few and he lived a very healthy life. Neither the polluted air, nor the chlorinated water could raise his hairline and he made it a habit to exercise and read his newspaper every day, even during his most hectic day. And the cells in his body saluted the man for his will-power and dedication.

"He aced the exams and joined one of the Big 4 accounting firms right away, and that deepened the wounds of his heart. Every night he returned home after 12 and left for work before 8.am. and spent the rest of the day in his daily chores like cleaning and washing. Kanha ensured that he spent no time idle and only such a hectic schedule kept the depression from licking off his heart and brain. But even if he sat back for a single second… he would reflect upon his past, think about this and that and from some unknown corner of his brain a stench will arise. He kept something hidden in the deepest cells of his brain and even I, his conscience, could not read it.

"One evening as he drove from work to home a little earlier than usual, he decided to stop by Marina beach and enjoy the breeze. But as the breeze soothed his skin outside, a thousand nails seemed to pierce it from inside. Two drops of tears rolled down his cheek and walked towards the incoming waves. He did not stop walking."

As I finished reading the compilation of his past, I walked over to talk to one of his older conscience and asked him, "You mentioned about Kanha thinking of nothing but his goals in life. Can you tell me what the goals are?"

"Nothing big, one of them replied."

"Get good marks for his exam. Be a successful person. Earn a good living. Just the regular stuff, that's all."

I felt like defenestrating them and setting their souls on fire. Kanha's goal – to earn a good living? "Did anyone even brush through my report?" I asked them all angrily and they stared at me blankly. Ignoring my own rhyme I said, "What kind of guidance are you going to give if you don't even know whom you are dealing with? Eight of you losers have repeatedly mentioned of his depression and sadness and not even one of you made a sincere effort to find what caused this sorrow. Losers. Never repeat this!" I shouted and marched away. I flew through the Portal and reached the hospital to find that Kanha was waking up.

"So, what is going on?" I entered his body and asked the brain.

"Ahh... long time no see. I thought I would never see you again."

"Literally. What was it with the life and death drama? I thought you had control."

"I do. This is the reason he was driving a car from office to his apartment when all this happened. As for the suicide, Kanha took control."

"Has it ever happened before?"

"No. As a matter of fact only now did I know that Kanha can act without my help. It was scary!"

Apparently the soul had taken control of Kanha's body instead of delegating it to the brain like it always did. "And do you know why he did that? What made him hate life so much?"

"No idea", the brain said simply and that response angered me. I dived into the brain and swam through the pool of his memories, most of which consisted of figures and facts relating to his clients at office. I went in deeper, digging through his childhood days and pulling out thoughts and ideas that he had kept secret from me too. And finally, I pulled out the cause of all this trauma, 'Kanha's Ambitions'. The brain itself had forgotten, that it possessed such a memory. And when it was reminded of it, it tried to shut down the memory completely, pushing it away from the conscious part of the brain, trying to put it away before Kanha was fully awake. But I knew that this was the only memory that caused him so much trouble. "No, put it away!" The brain screamed.

"You rascal! You are supposed to work for Kanha, not just kill his ambitions to suit your convenience. You are the reason Kanha is in the hospital today."

"Dev", the brain argued, "You know very well why I did it. These are not practicable thoughts, these are just stupid and I don't want Kanha to wander away again. Right now he is living a successful and peaceful life and that is enough."

Kanha was wriggling in his bed, violently shaking his head as he tried to suppress the unbearable pain. But I couldn't care less – the pain will die soon but I won't let Kanha live a life of such depression.

"The things that are in that memory are laughable, even Kanha will laugh at them, you yourself have laughed at them. They were a child's dreams, it has no purpose to serve in the adult world." The brain argued vehemently.

"Sometimes Kanha is wrong and sometimes you are wrong. That is what I am here for, to set your path right. And if that means I have to kill your maturity and turn you back into a toddler again, then I will do it!"

I pulled the memory from within his brain and threw it at his thoughts. Kanha woke up screaming in pain.

Had this happened a few years back I might have sided with the brain and killed the memory. But experience has taught me time and again that 'Maturity' is the real villain and if you even have to opportunity to be a kid throughout, even if it is at the cost of being labelled 'Mentally Handicapped', Go Ahead!

Kanha's throbbing head buzzed with activity, with the issues relating to office and his clients on one side and that of his childhood dreams on the other. His brain tried to convince him, "You know what is important. You know what the issues are. You are the star at office and you have to keep it up. Just remove every other thought from your brain." The brain instructed Kanha. Usually I would have stepped in and argued against him but this time I simply decided to sit back and watch. I knew that Kanha would handle it on his own.

His brain buzzed and the sound was almost audible in his ears. The numbers and data fought amongst themselves as they required clarification, and his ambitions fought their way to grab his undivided attention. I watched the fight scene carefully, thinking of when to intervene, and whether I have to intervene at all. Eventually I got bored and stepped into the scene.

"Numbers and figures and cases and office and work and files. Good job Kanha! You are doing such an amazing job, learning so much. Can you just tell me for what you are putting so much effort? And is this effort enough."

The brain screamed from the other direction, "Distraction is only for losers Kanha. Focus!" But my words found their mark. "Why all this hard work? For what purpose? And is this hard-work enough? No, I can very well answer the third question – No. I need to work harder, I have always taken an oath to work harder. But why?" Man, I am awesome. Once again I held up the ambitions list and showed it to him. And he read it carefully.

1. Ensure degree education for all the people in the nation.
2. Make sure that no human goes to bed hungry.
3. Every person must love the other like her very own brother or sister.
4. Nations that are at war must reconcile and live peacefully.

Kanha looked at the list and at first laughed at the list. It appears to be like one that was brought to their lands from Hogwarts. Slowly he recovered his memories and the attachment he felt for the list. During his teenage, the list was not just a dream or a vision but a tangible goal towards which he put an effort every night. He had spent many years in thinking of plans to achieve the goals and he wondered as to how to put his plans into action. And every morning he woke up with a fear – a fear that one day he might forget his list.

"You ponder about it yourself, while I attend to some other business", I told him and went away. Kanha could manage things on his own. He was an adult and his mother was right by his bed almost all night. "Speaking of which, how is he going to explain the suicide attempt to his mother. That is a crisis even I can't help him through!"

I made my way through the western ghats and vast rural lands to reach the spectacular metro, which hosts umpteen malls and cafes and cinema and everything else that would comprise the definition of a metro and yet I chose to visit the place which might be the only solace for anyone who prefers clean air to a disco-theque – The Indian Institute of Technology, Madras.

It was rather easy to find the girl doing her PhD in Development Studies, a dark skinned short girl with curly hair that hid a feather in it, and lovely eyes sticking her nose into one of the books that was certainly heavier than she was.

"Why are you so far away from him?" I asked her, hoping to get a response from her conscience. I tried to read her mind and found no thought of Kanha in them but her memories of Kanha were still fresh. "He needs you. I have to get you both back together", I said to myself and sat with her listening to her thoughts for some time and felt happy that she thought along the same lines as Kanha did. Apparently she was doing some research on the upliftment and protection of crippled beggars in the city, and it seemed she was making great strides. The research had taken her out of the library to the heart of the city of slum dwellers and pedlars and other dispossessed people of the city. She studied their lives and constituted a team that worked on taking them out of... whatever you call the place they are in right now. The sights of the city, where beggars, finger-less, stunted, burnt, living on the foot-paths was one that pained every city dwellers eyes. Most of them had trained themselves to ignore such eye-sores and focus on the temple that stood behind these homeless men and women. Radha, being the girl she was wouldn't do such a thing.

I stood up to give her a salute and decided to glide away just when I noticed a miraculous sight. The white feather emerged from her head and flew off into the sky. "So she has finally got rid of it. That is one reason to celebrate!"

I glided outside the library and slowly moved along the forest campus enjoying the scenery that surrounded me, and again the white feather that flew out of Radha's head caught my eyes. "Wonder if she knows that she has finally got rid of that feather?" I said and saw the feather go higher and higher. Defying the laws of gravity as if it had come from my world, from the after-life... BLOODY BLUNDALEOMITE!

I blasted to grab the feather but couldn't get hold of it as it continued to go higher and higher until it reached the clouds and entered it. I followed the feather's trail and saw the feather unleash its true form, transforming into a tall man with muscular features. And to greet him, a short man appeared out of nowhere and the two embraced. Only after they let go of each other did they notice that their privacy had been invaded.

"I don't think it was such a good thing you are up to", I told them both and saw the colour drain from their faces. Not literally because souls don't have blood and they just glow in blue and white, but their face showed a similar expression. Kind of like, "Busted!"

"What do you mean?" The short fellow tried to manage the scene. "What are you talking about?"

"Hey, I know you", suddenly I recognised the man I had caught red handed. "You are the one who was thrown out of the firm for some mischief right? The rogue conscience. Doesn't seem you have any intention of mending your ways."

"None of your business", the tall fellow said in a thick belligerent voice but it wouldn't work on me. I countered him in an intense tone, "It does concern me because you have been spying on Radha. That too for a very long time. Interesting, stick to somebody's head in the form of a feather. But it seemed you chose the wrong neighbourhood to mess around."

The two men looked stumped, rather two faced. On one hand they were worried that I would create unnecessary and maybe even some severe problems. While on the other hand it irritated them that their most ambitious project was facing a hitch from some puny conscience.

"Well then, shall I report my suspicion right away or do you wish to have a hearing. An opportunity to present your case before I ruin everything you have been doing. And I hope you are not doing the mistake of under-estimating me. You see, whatever it is you are up to, I am sure I can ruin things." Some souls block their minds from being read, but whatever skill they possessed, I could tell whether they were right or wrong. That was the only reason I didn't alert Praveen right away. There was something good behind them.

As the two of them had an intense discussion on how to get rid of me (saying a lie was not an option, I could find out. They could try and compromise some of the story and hope of convincing me, but there was uncertainity as to how much they should tell me), I closed my eyes, giving them the signal that I would contact Praveen any moment. "Wait wait, don't ruin it, we will tell you."

"The whole story", I demanded with my eyes closed, my mind so close to touching Praveen.

"Fine. But you must promise to keep it a secret!"

"I can only decide that once I have heard the story."

"You very well know that there is only good in the after-life. We got busted for breaking the law, not for doing anything bad", the short man tried to sell a story.

"I have seen an anti-conscience, your bluff won't work on me", my eyes were still closed.

"Alright. Then you have to promise that you will not tell the story to anyone if you feel we are just. That is a fair deal", that was indeed a fair deal. And I was pretty sure I was about to hear a good story. And that story was inexplicably intertwined with Kanha's life.

"Deal!"

And the feather man began narrating his story, "This story happened five thousand years ago: Sita woke up when the moon was still full in the sky...", and after a full hour the story ended with, "He held the lifeless body of Sita close to his chest and screamed out the very last drop of air from within him."

With a blank face I asked them, "What does this story have to do with anything?"

"So it seems we have to tell you everything", the short man, Karn as I recall his name, let a sigh which meant those words. He spoke, "Do you believe in destiny?"

I gave them an outright, "NO." Such a ridiculous concept yaar, destiny says that everything that happens in the world is already written down somewhere and everything that happens in the universe is just as said in that book. So what does that make all of us? What is the point of all this guidance and life and hard-work, if no matter what you do you are going to get what has been written, nothing more nothing less. The idea of destiny defeated the purpose of life.

"You have got it all wrong", Karn read my thoughts and responded. "Destiny is not a book that dictates the law. Destiny isn't a novel or a story as you imagine it to be. It is a set of questions that humans have to answer.

"Destiny does not say whether such a thing will happen or not", Karn elaborated. "Such a thing will happen, he will win, he will lose, none of that is written in the Destiny. Destiny simply asks certain questions, "Do you choose to be honest?", "Do you choose to pick a weapon or fight peacefully?" and such stuff. It basically gives structure to life.

"Destiny has a role in deciding what you become in life, not by dictating terms but by asking question. If Destiny wants a certain person to become a doctor, "Are you ready to work hard?", "Do you want to learn about the human body?", but eventually it is only our choices that make us who we are.

"However", he continued after a pause, "the Destiny has preferences. While it asks you, "Do you want to sing or dance?" and leaves the choice completely open to you, there is a certain answer that Destiny prefers. On giving the right answer, the person is rewarded. On giving the wrong answer, a person is punished. And sometimes a moderate answer will neither bless or curse, but simply alter our future by throwing at us a different set of questions in the days to come. Those questions which require a correct answer; that is where we come into play – the Conscience.

"We are equipped with a deep knowledge of the world and its laws, the way it works, about what is right and what is not, and we are the closest to destiny. Most often, our advices are in line with Destiny's preferred lines."

There was another pause and I stared at them emotionlessly. Not because there was no emotion, but because I was way too engrossed in their story. Reading my face, Karn continued, "So we got a little greedy and decided to have a peak at destiny. Somehow access the secrets of destiny and that will turn out to be the biggest blessing for all of us conscience. I mean, instead of so much studying and hard work, we could simply turn the pages of destiny and find out what we are supposed to do.

"Okay, let me admit, our intentions were too greedy and shrewd when we decided to steal the book. We wanted to be the best conscience in all of after-life, taking us that much closer to…" Karn let the sentence trail and I didn't complain.

"But our attempt was a tragic failure and as a punishment we were thrown out of the firm. The office declared that we were never ever again to become the conscience of any soul, ever! This happened more than 5,000 years back. After that, the two of us were out on the streets of after-life looking for a job. That is when Prith, my friend over here came up with this idea. We had done so much research and studies on destiny, so why not further pursue our research in a just manner. No stealing, no robbery, nothing of the sort.

"We decided to study Destiny and recreate our own version of the book that would be in-line with the real destiny. We can't become a conscience now, this is the least we can do for our profession."

"Re-create destiny?" I asked.

"For that, we decided to observe the lives and times of some people and look at the way their lives progressed. For every sin they did, how did the Destiny punish them, for every act of kindness, how did the Destiny reward them. The job was herculean and would take millennia to complete, we knew, but then we decided to go ahead with it. And we are almost complete", Karn announced and pulled a gigantic book out of thin air. The cover read the words, "Simple Guide to Become a Successful Conscience!"

I stretched my arms but Karn suddenly pulled the book away. "No, no, no... It is not complete yet."

"Alright", I had two more doubts and it continued to prick me. "You want to write about destiny, you are spying on Radha and the story of that ancient girl Sita. What does all this have to do with anything?"

Karn answered with a sly smile. "Five thousand years ago we decided to keep an eye on the life times of a girl, the first step of our task. That girl was Sita. After she died that night, she was taken to heaven straight away, but she refused to go. She wanted to go back to earth."

The scene was becoming intense and Karn weighed each of his words very carefully. "Why?" I asked.

"Two reasons", Karn replied. "She had failed in her life on two counts. One to establish the strength and supremacy of Ahimsa over violence. And the second, to find her lost love and live a full life with him."

"I remember the words she said as the gates of heaven opened before her", Prith quoted Sita, "If I am to ever enter these gates, it will only be with my head resting on his shoulders."

"And Adithya, what happened to him?"

"His fault was not so great that it deserved punishment and he too was taken into afterlife. But the first thing he asked them was what happened to Sita.

They informed him of her decision and he too asked for a re-incarnation." Karn and Prith looked at each other and sighed.

"What happened? What happened after that?" I asked eagerly.

"Their births never coincided", Karn said with a sorrow filled voice. "He was born as a dog and she as a cat. Him as a snake and she as a mongoose and finally when both of them where reincarnated as humans, Adithya died two days after Sita was born. Not once in these five thousand years did their births coincide!" There was a sense of frustration in his voice.

"Why? I mean, that sounds a little strange. Even reincarnation comes under the purview of Destiny right?"

"What happened five thousand years ago was not just an ordinary love story, it was the first victory of violence over non-violence! That night Adithya chose his sword and decided to shed blood. He won the battle and established a kingdom over there and ruled many lands during his life. And he was a truly great king, not just a conqueror, but a real king. He was merciful, kind and ensured equality and fraternity among his people. But his choice...

"Just as Sita had predicted that night, His choice echoed for generations to come. If Adithya picked up the sword for love, his sons picked it up for friendship, their sons picked it up for honour and their children picked it up for money and fame. Violence crept into the hearts and minds of people throughout the world. The idea that anyone with force can establish his dominance over the other was accepted by all. The idea that you can repay any pain with violence was one every human accepted warmly. Fight for love, fight for hate, fight for money and sex. Youngsters think it is cool. Killing became a sport. Mankind almost adopted Cannibalism.

"It may not have been intentional, but all of that was Adithya's doing, you have to admit. And if I am not wrong, this is how destiny chose to punish him."

"What should he do to have salvation?"

"Undo whatever he did. Declare the victory of non-violence over violence."

"But it happened. India's struggle for independence. It was the victory of Ahimsa."

"That was a truly great victory. But for him to have salvation everything he did must be reversed. How happily did everyone accept the idea of violence. Adithya must do something that makes people accept the idea of non-violence just as happily."

"They are still waiting for each other?" I asked Karn and Prith.

A smile emerged from Karn's face, "Not anymore. Finally, it has coincided. They are both humans of the same age right now. And this is his only chance to win!"

"Huh?" I didn't understand the last sentence.

"Adithya has tried way too many times, but never succeeded. According to my calculations, he will be able to succeed only with the support of his Sita!"

So their story was about to come to an end. "And Sita is re-incarnated as Radha?" I guessed.

"Exactly", Prith the feather who has been stalking her for millennia, confirmed.

To attain salvation he will have to change the world. Brotherhood, love, world peace... Everything fit in! "I will have Kanha come over right away, no matter what I have to do. He will meet Radha today itself."

"Who?" Karn looked confused.

"Kanha. My human. He is Adithya's re-incarnation right?"

"Oh... that boy. No, no, he isn't Adithya."

"What!?" That seemed absurd to me. "Not possible. If Kanha isn't Adithya then where is Adithya? And who is Kanha?"

"To your second question you have a very proud answer. Kanha is the re-incarnation of Adithya's conscience!"

That was an awesome thing to hear. "When Adithya chose the sword, the one who suffered the biggest failure. Your Kanha has also come back to redeem himself."

"What else do you know about Kanha?" I asked.

"Just this much. And that this failure of his was the only reason he was denied entry to heaven."

"And where is Adithya?"

The look turned grave on their faces. "We don't know", Karn said flatly. "We have looked for him everywhere but no use. We are sure that he is somewhere around, but where exactly? We are still looking for him."

The fact that someone from afterlife cannot track a particular human was odd. Even mobile network people can do that with a flick of their fingers. However, much more than that was going through my mind, much bigger things to finish and I made a dash for it. "Okay great, thanks. And good luck with the book. By the way, one last question, why did you make me promise that I shouldn't tell the story to anyone?"

"We want the book release to be a big surprise", both of them said proudly.

I dived towards earth in a flash and reached Kanha's side. He was being fed porridge and was slowly recovering. I couldn't stand the excitement of all the news I had just heard and couldn't wait to talk about it to Kanha. That evening as the lights were turned off and Kanha struggled to find some sleep, I spoke to him. "So what do you think about your ambitions?"

"The list? That was just a childhood joke. How can anyone take it seriously? World peace, as if. I am struggling to find some peace in my home."

"Childhood joke? Kanha, you really think that the things you wrote in that list was a joke? Do you think it was childish? Kanha, whatever you wrote in that piece of memory was something even the greatest leaders of the world fear to talk about. At such a young age you had sown the seeds of deep and powerful ambition. And the severity of your desire was nothing like I had ever seen. Kanha, not every person has dreams like you. When you have dreams, go ahead and get it!"

"What non-sense? What about my job? What about my career?"

"Yes you can do that. Your work and your career, pursue it with every drop of energy in your body. But answer me Kanha, is that all you are capable of?"

Kanha did not respond, so I continued, "The Kanha I knew was capable of miracles. He created wonders. He was a wonder child. And now look at you. You are just another auditor. Just another auditor."

"I do my work with perfection."

"There are millions of homeless hungry people in the country who live lives that is literally disgusting.

So many of them in Chennai itself, Kanha how could you turn a blind eye towards them? How can you live peacefully when you don't answer your calling? How can you ever be happy if your heart is not satisfied?"

"You are bluffing."

"No matter how hard you work, no matter what you achieve, you will not feel content, you will not feel satisfied, not unless you re-open that list and go ahead with it."

"I don't even know where to start from", Kanha's head was aching again.

"Has that ever been an excuse?" I asked and quit the scene. I was sure that Kanha would come up with an answer, but that will never be the right answer so I itself decided against myself to help him out. "Find Radha", I whispered and vanished.

The next day he searched Radha on Facebook and discovered that she was doing her PhD in IIT Madras. He looked up their mutual friends and noticed a couple of people whose mobile number he had. He rang them up, exchanged pleasantries and acquired Radha's phone number. Early morning itself he phoned her and before the third ring she picked up the phone, "Hello?" her voice was melodious. Kanha stuttered and went speechless. Speak up you moron, I shouted at him.

"Hi. Radha?"

"Yes, may I know who is speaking?"

"This is Kanha."

That day itself he got discharged from the hospital and caught a bus to Madras and the next morning he found himself in the sprawling magnificent campus of IITM. "Such a long time, how are you?" Radha did not hide her excitement at the sight of her best friend. Her best friend forever.

"You never call. What can I do?" Kanha commented and Radha laughed.

"What brings you around these places?" Radha asked, and Kanha explained to her about his job and his life at Chennai and expressed his regrets at not being able to meet her before. "So how are you?"

"Same old same old", Radha answered with a laugh. Her curly tufts looked pretty on her dark face. And IIT had gifted her with glasses which went very well with her character.

"How are your friends over here?" Kanha asked.

"You have always known Kanha, that you were my only real friend." She smiled and added, "there are a bunch of girls. Hostel-mates, team-mates and all that. I never feel lonely."

"I have been brutally depressed for the past few days. Never had any friends and the only one I have is... I seriously messed up our friendship didn't I." I noticed that Kanha was speaking at a level of emotional intelligence that went way beyond his normal capabilities. So loneliness does things to you. "Can we talk?" Kanha asked and Radha led him to a little spot behind her hostel under a tree where nobody was around. The two of them sat on the protruding roots of the tree and Kanha burst open.

He revealed himself like he had never before. As a matter of fact he had not opened to me either the way he talked to Radha. He told her about how narrow minded he was throughout school and how nothing else occupied his mind but studies and the how during his senior secondary school days there was a shift of gear and it was almost as if he had been possessed. Then he told her about his life after school, about how he was rather successful in life, yet so depressed. Then finally he revealed the last piece of his secret. "When I was a kid I was really ambitious! I had a dream that I must do something that would fully eradicate poverty from the world, how I would spread education to the deprived people of the world and all that. And now, all of it seems so laughable."

"Not so laughable if you ask me. Rather admirable."

"You have always been so kind to me", Kanha smiled at her. "So what are you doing these days?"

"Eradicating poverty", she said with a giggle. Kanha looked at her dubiously, making sure she wasn't making fun of him, "No seriously. I am doing a research on beggars and we are doing a project for the upliftment of slum dwellers and beggars in the city. Not as extensive as your list, but we are doing it in our own small ways."

"Can I join the team?"

"Huh?"

"To help you guys out. As a volunteer or an additional team member or a helping hand, just for the satisfaction. Just for the learning experience."

"We actually need quite a few helping hands. Let me just ask my —"

"Please do that and let me know. No fees, no credits… And don't think of this as a payback for all that you have done for me." He smiled and stood up. The new Kanha astounded Radha and she sat there with her jaw dropped.

"So why didn't you tell me about Kanha's previous incarnations?" I asked Praveen one evening during one of our random conversations.

"What previous incarnation?"

"Not his incarnation actually. I am more concerned about his work as a conscience." Praveen looked up at me with a serious look and seemed a little disappointed that I had come to know. "How did you come to know?", he asked.

"I promised the source that this question will not be answered. However, that is not important is it? Why didn't you tell me?"

Praveen sighed and replied, "Kanha's failure as a conscience was something huge. His failure changed the world and it was not such a good change. For years he slogged with us in disgrace. It is only now that he finally got an opportunity to mend his mistakes and he wanted to do it on his own. Without the help of a conscience even. But according to our rules we have to depute a conscience to every human so he asked us to send the worst souls to the job."

"Excuse me?" I mean, that was rude right?

"No offence Dev, but I put you on job right away remember. You were not given any training, any practice, no senior to guide you or anything, you were simply thrown into the well. And if you look at it, we have very selectively sent the dumbest of souls to conscience him after you."

"Yes, I noticed that. But I don't think it is a wise thing to do."

"I understand. You can stick around for a while yourself and set things straight as much as possible.

Kanha has a long way to go, so much to do, and he better start already."

"I have set things in motion. Now we he will carry things forward on his own and if he ever thinks of stopping, we can give him a nice pat."

"Good!" Praveen said with a smile.

"Again it seems so strange right", I asked curiously. "A boy with such a normal childhood, living an ordinary life, happens to be the one who has changed the world. And the same guy is going to change the world again. I mean, I didn't have any clue that he was somebody of this stature..."

"Everybody is Dev. Every childhood is just like this one, every soul is just like this. Every person has the potential for greatness, the fire to change the world. The great men are not earmarked, they are one among us, always around us. They just... choose to go the extra mile."

"And Radha? Her story is so..."

"She has two missions in hand. First, she must have Adithya choose to drop the sword. Second, and most importantly, she has to find Adithya."

"Where is Adithya?"

"Wherever he is, it is not going to be easy to find out. Radha will have to put her strengths to the test, go beyond every limit, overtake every horizon if she has to win this game. And there is no choice but victory, they have waited for 5000 years."

"What do you think will happen in the end?"

"Happily ever after. That is for sure. They might fail in this lifetime too, you never know, but one day they will succeed. Radha has the most powerful weapons in her hands, Ahimsa and Love. They are slow but when they succeed, it is like nothing else."

"And do you think the world will change. All of the them, the politicians, the dictators, the bureaucrats, and all the other people. Do you think corruption, poverty, illiteracy and all that will be wiped off the planet?" Optimism was always my greatest strength, but such questions merited doubt even from my side.

"Isn't that our purpose? The purpose of every soul. To bring about happiness and peace to the world. And remove anything that comes in between, be it corruption, poverty or whatever."

I looked up at the thousands of stars that shined in the sky that night and felt happy. Nobody knew what would happen in the end, but wasn't that the fun part after all. And only this ignorance could give you the opportunity to hope. Nahh... I have no doubts now. Sita and Adithya, Radha and whatever his name is, they will come together, Kanha will change the world and most importantly, there will be happiness.

*In the mountains there was little mercy. The people didn't have mercy, nature didn't have mercy, the government didn't have mercy and the soldiers were absolutely brutal. Nobody remembers who was right or who was wrong but the village had always revolted against the army which oppressed them and the army always tried to suppress them. "We are just doing what we can to protect the people", they argued.*

*The youth were divided. Some decided to flee the village, some decided to sit mum while some others decided to fight fire with fire. One night 8 college students set the military barracks on fire and bombed their armoury. 7 of them were shot dead during the attack itself, and only one of them managed to escape. He caught the first train that arrived at the station and set off to some unknown land, with nothing to survive on except one oath – "I will be back for justice!"*